The Bobbsey Twins
at School

D0826527

The Bobbsey Twins
at School

by Laura Lee Hope

Wilder Publications, LLC.
PO Box 3005
Radford VA 24143-3005

ISBN 10: 1-61720-306-8
ISBN 13: 978-1-61720-306-0

Table of Contents:

A Circus Train. . . . . · · · 7
Snoop Is Gone . . . . · · · 14
A Queer Dog . . . . · · · 19
Home in an Auto . . . . · · · 23
Snap Does Tricks. . . . . · · · 28
Danny Rugg Is Mean. . . . . · · · 32
At School . . . . · · · 36
Bert Sees Something . . . . · · · 41
Off to the Woods. . . . . · · · 45
A Scare . . . . · · · 50
Danny's Trick . . . . · · · 55
The Children's Party. . . . . · · · 60
An Unpleasant Surprise. . . . . · · · 64
A Coat Button . . . . · · · 68
Thanksgiving. . . . . · · · 74
Mr. Tetlow Asks Questions. . . . . · · · 78
The First Snow. . . . . · · · 82
A Night Alarm . . . . · · · 86
Who Was Smoking?. . . . . · · · 90
A Confession. . . . . · · · 94
The Fat Lady's Letter.. . . . . · · · 97
Snap and Snoop.. . . . . · · · 100

A Circus Train

"Mamma, how much longer have we got to ride?" asked Nan Bobbsey, turning in her seat in the railroad car, to look at her parents, who sat behind her.

"Are you getting tired?" asked Nan's brother Bert. "If you are I'll sit next to the window, and watch the telegraph poles and trees go by. Maybe that's what tires you, Nan," he added, and his father smiled, for he saw that Bert had two thoughts for himself, and one for his sister.

"No, I'm not tired of the scenery," answered the brownhaired and browneyed girl, "but you may sit next the window, Bert, if you like."

"Thanks!" he exclaimed as he scrambled over to the place his sister gave up.

"Are you tired, dearie?" asked Mrs. Bobbsey, leaning forward and smoothing out her daughter's hair with her hand. "If you would like to sit with me and put your head in my lap, papa can go to another seat and—"

"Oh, no, mamma, I'm not as tired as that," and Nan laughed. "I was just wondering how soon we'd be home."

"I'd rather be back at the seashore," said Bert, not turning his gaze from the window, for the train was passing along some fields just then, and in one a boy was driving home some cows to be milked, as evening was coming on. Bert was wondering if one of the cows might not chase the boy. Bert didn't really want to see the boy hurt by a cow, of course, but he thought that if the cow was going to take after the boy, anyhow, he might just as well see it. But the cows were very well-behaved, and went along slowly.

"Yes, the seashore was nice," murmured Nan, as she leaned her head back on the cushioned seat, "but I'm glad to be going home again. I want to see some of the girls, and—"

"Yes, and I'll be looking for some of the boys, too," put in Bert. "But school will soon begin, and that's no fun!"

Mr. and Mrs. Bobbsey smiled at each other, and Mr. Bobbsey, taking out a timetable, looked to see how much longer they would be on the train.

"It's about an hour yet," he said to Nan, and she sighed. Really she was more tired than she cared to let her mother know.

Just ahead of the two Bobbsey children were another set of them. I say "set" for the Bobbsey children came "in sets."

There were two pairs of twins, Bert and Nan, nearly nine years of age, and Flossie and Freddie, almost five. And, whereas the two older children were rather tall and slim, with dark brown hair and eyes, the littler twins were short and fat, and had light hair and blue eyes. The two pairs of twins were quite a contrast, and many persons stopped to look at them as they passed along the street together.

"No, sir," went on Bert musingly, "school's no fun, and it starts about a week after we get home. No chance to have a good time!"

"We've had fun all summer," replied his sister. "I rather like school."

"Mamma, are we going to school this year?" asked Flossie, as she looked back with a quick turning of her head that set her yellow curls to dancing.

"If we are, I'm going to sit with Flossie—can't I?" asked Freddie, kneeling in the seat so that he could face back to his father and mother.

Indeed his request was not strange, since the two younger twins were always together even more so than their brother and sister.

"Yes, I think you and Freddie will start school regularly this term," said Mrs. Bobbsey, "and, if it can be arranged, you may sit together. We'll see about that. Be careful, Freddie, don't put your head out of the window," she cautioned quickly, for the little chap had turned in his seat again, and was leaning forward to see a horse galloping about a field, kicking up its heels at the sound of the puffing engine.

"It's my turn to sit by the window, anyhow," said Flossie.

"It is not! We haven't passed a station yet," disputed Freddie.

"Oh, we have so!" cried his little sister. "Freddie Bobbsey!" and she pointed her finger at him.

"Children—children," said Mrs. Bobbsey, reprovingly.

"Are you two taking turns?" asked Bert, smiling with an older brother's superior wisdom.

"Yes," answered Flossie, "he was to have the seat next to the window until we came to a station, and then it's to be my turn until we pass another station, and we have passed one, but he won't change over."

"Well, it was only a little station, anyhow," asserted Freddie, "and it came awful quick after the last one. It isn't fair!"

"There's a seat up ahead for you, Bert," suggested Mr. Bobbsey, as a gentleman got up, when the train approached a station. "You can sit there, and let Flossie or Freddie take your place."

"All right," answered Bert goodnaturedly, as he got up.

The train rolled on, the two younger twins each having a window now, and Nan occupying the seat with her little brother. For a time there was quietness, until Mrs. Bobbsey said to her husband:

"Hadn't you better get some of the satchels together, Richard, and tell Dinah what she is to carry?"

"I think I will," he answered, as he went up the car aisle a little way to where a very fat colored woman sat. She was Dinah, the Bobbsey cook, and they took her with them always when going away for the summer. Now they were on their way to their city house, and of course Dinah came back, too.

"Mamma, I'm thirsty," said Flossie, after a bit. "Please may I get a drink?"

"I want one, too," said Freddie quicky. "Come on, Flossie, we'll both go down to the end of the car where the water cooler is."

"There's no cup," Nan said. "I went a little while ago, but a lady let me take her glass."

"And if there was a cup, I would rather they didn't use it," said Mrs. Bobbsey. "One never knows who has last handled a public cup."

"But I want a drink," insisted Flossie, a bit fretfully, for she was tired from the long journey.

"I know it, dear," said her mamma gently, "and I'm getting out the silver cup for you. Only you must be very careful of it, and not drop it, for it is solid silver and will dent, or mar, easily." She was searching in her bag, and presently took out a very valuable drinking cup, gold lined and with much engraving on it. The cup had been presented to Flossie and Freddie on their first birthday, and bore each of their names. They were very proud of it.

"Now be careful," warned Mrs. Bobbsey, as she held out the cup. "Hold on to the seats as you walk along."

"I'll carry the cup," said Freddie. "I'm the biggest."

"You are not!" declared his sister quickly. "I'm just as big."

"Well, anyhow, I'm a boy," went on Freddie, and Flossie could not deny this. "And boys always carries things," her brother went on. "I'll carry the cup."

"Very well, but be careful of it," said his mother with a smile, as she handed it to him. The two children went down the aisle of the car. They stopped for a moment at the seat where Dinah was.

"Is Snoop all right?" asked Freddie, peering into a box that was made of slats, with spaces between them for air.

"'Deed an' he am, honey," said Dinah with a smile, laughing so that she shook all over her big, fleshy body.

"I 'specs he's lonesome; aren't you, Snoop?" asked Flossie, poking her finger in one of the cracks, to caress, as well as she could, a fat, black cat. The cat, like Dinah the cook, went with the Bobbseys on all their summer outings.

"Well, maybe he am lonesome," admitted Dinah, with another laugh, "but he's been real good. He hadn't yowled once—not once!"

"He'll soon be out of his cage; won't you, Snoop?" said Freddie, and then he and his sister went on to the water cooler. Near it they saw something else to look at. This was the sight of a very, very fat lady who occupied nearly all of one seat in the end of the car. She was so large that only a very little baby could have found room beside her.

"Look—look at her," whispered Flossie to Freddie, as they paused. The fat woman's back was toward them, and she seemed to be much interested in looking out of the window.

"She is fat," admitted Freddie. "Did you ever see one so big before?"

"Only in a circus," said Flossie.

"She'd make make two of Dinah," went on her brother.

"She would not," contradicted Flossie quickly. "'Cause Dinah's black, and this lady is white."

"That's so," admitted Freddie, with smile. "I didn't think of that."

A sway of the train nearly made Flossie fall, and she caught quickly at her brother.

"Look out!" he cried. "You 'mos knocked the cup down."

"I didn't mean to," spoke Flossie. "Oh, there goes my hat! Get it, Freddie, before someone steps on it!"

Her brother managed to get the hat just as it was sliding under the seat where the fat lady sat.

After some confusion the hat was placed on Flossie's head, and once more she and her brother moved on toward the water cooler. It was getting dusk now, and some of the lamps in the car had been lighted.

Freddie, carrying the cup, filled it with water at the little faucet, and, very politely, offered it to his sister first. Freddie was no better than most boys of his age, but he did not forget some of the little polite ways his mamma was continually teaching him. One of these was "ladies first," though Freddie did not always carry it out, especially when he was in a hurry.

"Do you want any more?" he asked, before he would get himself a drink.

"Just a little," said Flossie. "The silver cup doesn't hold much."

"No, I guess it's 'cause there's so much silver in it," replied her brother. "It's worth a lot of money, mamma said."

"Yes, and it's all ours. When I grow up I'm going to have my half made into a bracelet."

"You are?" said Freddie slowly. "If you do there won't be enough left for me to drink out of."

"Well, you can have your share of it made into a watch, and drink out of a glass."

"That's so," agreed Freddie, his face brightening. He gave his sister more water, and then took some himself. As he drank his eyes were constantly looking at the very fat lady who filled so much of her seat. She turned from the window and looked at the two children, smiling broadly. Freddie was somewhat confused, and looked down quickly. Just then the train gave another lurch and Freddie suddenly spilled some of the water on his coat.

"Oh, look what you did!" cried Flossie. "And that's your best coat!"

"I—I couldn't help it," stammered Freddie.

"Never mind, little boy," said the fat lady. "It's only clean water. Come here and I'll wipe it off with my handkerchief. I'd come to you, only I'm so stout it's hard enough for me to walk anyhow, and when the train is moving I simply can't do it."

Freddie and Flossie went to her seat, and with a handkerchief, that Flossie said afterward was almost as big as a table cloth, the fat lady wiped the water off Freddie's coat.

The little boy held the silver cup in his hand, and feeling, somehow, that he ought to repay the fat lady's kindness in some way, after thanking her, he asked:

"Would you like a drink of water? I can bring it to you if you would."

"Thank you," she answered. "What a kind little boy you are! I saw you give your sister a drink first, too. Yes, I would like a drink. I've been wanting one some time, but I didn't dare get up to go after it."

"I'll get it!" cried Freddie, eager to show what a little man he was. He made his way to the cooler without accident, and then, moving slowly, taking hold of the seat on the way back, so as not to spill the water, he brought the silver cup brimful to the fat lady.

"Oh, what a beautiful cup," she said, as she took it.

"And it cost a lot of money, too," said Flossie. "It's ours—our birthday cup, and when I grow up I'm going to have a bracelet made from my half."

"That will be nice," said the fat lady, as she prepared to drink.

But she never got more than a sip of the water Freddie had so kindly brought her, for, no sooner did her lips touch the cup than there was a

grinding, shrieking sound, a jar to the railway coach, and the train came to such a sudden stop that many passengers were thrown from their seats.

Flossie and Freddie sat down suddenly in the aisle, but they were so fat that they did not mind it in the least. As surprised as he was, Freddie noticed that the fat lady was so large that she could not be thrown out of her seat, no matter how suddenly the train stopped. The little Bobbsey boy saw the water from the cup spill all over the fat lady, and she held the silver vessel in her big, pudgy hand, looking curiously at it, as though wondering what had so quickly become of the water.

"It's a wreck—the train's off the track!" a man exclaimed.

"We've hit something!" cried another.

"It's an accident, anyhow," said still a third, and then every one seemed to be talking at once.

Mr. Bobbsey came running down the aisle to where Flossie and Freddie still sat, dazed.

"Are you hurt?" he cried, picking them both up together, which was rather hard to do.

"No—no," said Freddie slowly.

"Oh, papa, what is it?" asked Flossie, wondering whether she was going to cry.

"I don't know, my dear. Nothing serious, I guess. The engineer must have put the brakes on too quickly. I'll look out and see."

Knowing that his children were safe, Mr. Bobbsey put them down and led them back to where his wife was anxiously waiting.

"They're all right," he called. "No one seems to be hurt."

Bert Bobbsey looked out of the window. Though darkness had fallen there seemed to be many lights up ahead of the stopped train. And in the light Bert could see some camels, an elephant or two, a number of horses, and cages containing lions and tigers strung out along the track.

"Why—why, what's this—a circus?" he asked. "Look, Nan! See those monkeys!"

"Why, it is a circus—and the train must have been wrecked!" exclaimed his sister. "Oh mamma, what can it be?"

A brakeman came into the car where the Bobbseys were.

"There's no danger," he said. "Please keep your seats. A circus train that was running ahead of us got off the track, and some of the animals are loose. Our train nearly ran into an elephant, and that's why the engineer had to stop so suddenly. We will go on I soon."

"A circus, eh?" said Mr. Bobbsey. "Well, well! This is an adventure, children. We've run into a circus train! Let's watch them catch the animals."

Snoop Is Gone

"Papa, do you think a tiger would come in here?" asked Freddie, remembering all the stories of wild animals he had heard in his four years.

"Or a lion?" asked Flossie.

"Of course not!" exclaimed Nan. "Can't you see that all the wild animals are still in their cages?"

"Maybe some of 'em are loose," suggested Freddie, and he almost hoped so, as long as his father was there to protect him.

"I guess the circus men can look after them," said Bert. "May I get off, father, and look around?"

"I'd rather you wouldn't, son. You can't tell what may happen."

"Oh, look at that man after the monkey!" cried Nan.

"Yes, and the monkey's gone up on top of the tiger's cage," added Bert. "Say, this is as good as a circus, anyhow!"

Some of the big, flaring lights, used in the tents at night, had been set going so the circus and railroad men could see to work, and this glare gave the Bobbseys and other passengers on the train a chance to see what was going on.

"There's a big elephant!" cried Freddie. "See him push the lion's cage around. Elephants are awful strong!"

"They couldn't push a railroad train," said Flossie.

"They could too!" cried her little brother, quickly.

"They could not. Could they, papa?"

"What?" asked Mr. Bobbsey, absentmindedly.

"Could an elephant push a railroad train?" asked Flossie.

"I know they could," declared Freddie. "Couldn't they, papa?"

"Now, children, don't argue. Look out of the windows," advised their mother.

And while the circus men are trying to catch the escaped animals I will tell you something more about the Bobbseys, and about the other books, before this one, relating to their doings.

Mr. Richard Bobbsey, and his wife Mary, the parents of the Bobbsey twins, lived in an Eastern city called Lakeport, on Lake Metoka. Mr. Bobbsey was in the lumber business, and the yard, with its great piles of logs and boards, was near the lake, on which the twins often went in boats. There was also a river running into the lake, not far from the saw mill.

Their house was about a quarter of a mile away from the lumber yard, on a fashionable street, and about it was a large lawn, while in the back Sam Johnson, the colored man of all work, and the husband of Dinah, had a fine garden. The Bobbseys had many vegetables from this garden.

There was also a barn near the house, and in this the children had many good times. Flossie and Freddie played there more than did Nan and Bert, who were growing too old for games of that sort.

As I have said, Bert and Nan were rather tall and thin, while Flossie and Freddie were short and fat. Mr. Bobbsey used often to call Flossie his "Fat Fairy," which always made her laugh. And Freddie had a pet name, too. It was "Fat Fireman," for he often played that he was a fireman; putting out makebelieve fires, and pretending he was a fire engine. Once or twice his father had taken him to see a real one, and this pleased Freddie very much.

In the first book of this series, called "The Bobbsey Twins," I told you something of the fun the four children had in their home town. They had troubles, too, and Danny Rugg, one of the few bad boys in Lakeport, was the cause of some. Also about a certain broken window; what happened when the twins went coasting, how they had a good time in an ice boat, and how they did many other things.

Snoop, the fat, black kitten, played a part in the story also. The Bobbsey twins were very fond of Snoop, and had kept him so many years that I suppose he ought to be called cat, instead of a kitten, now.

After the first winter's fun, told of in the book that began an account of the doings of the Bobbseys, the twins and their parents went to the home of Uncle Daniel Bobbsey, and his wife, Aunt Sarah, in Meadow Brook.

In the book called "The Bobbsey Twins in the Country," I wrote down many of the things that happened during the summer.

If they had fun going off to the country, taking Snoop with them, of course, they had many more good times on arriving at the farm. There was a picnic, jolly times in the woods, a Fourth of July celebration, and though a midnight scare alarmed them for a time, still they did not mind that.

But, though the twins liked the country very much, they soon had a chance to see something of the ocean, and in the third book of the series, called "The Bobbsey Twins at the Seashore," my readers will find out what happened there.

There was fun on the sand, and more fun in the water, and once the little ones got lost on an island. A great storm came up, and a ship was wrecked, and this gave the twins a chance to see the life savers, those brave men who risk their lives to help others.

Then came closing days at Ocean Cliff, the home of Uncle William and Aunt Emily Minturn at Sunset Beach. School was soon to open, and Mr. and Mrs. Bobbsey were anxious to get back to their town home, for Flossie and Freddie were to start regular lessons now, even though it was but in the kindergarten class.

So goodbyes were said to the ocean, and though Dorothy Minturn cried a little when her cousins Nan and Flossie, and Bert and Freddie, had to leave, still she said she hoped they would come again. And so the Bobbseys were on their way home in the train when the circus accident happened that brought them to a stop.

"And so we nearly ran into an elephant, eh?" said Mr. Bobbsey to the brakeman, who had brought in the news.

"Yes, sir. Our engineer stopped just in time."

"If we had hit him we'd gone off the track," said Freddy.

"No, we wouldn't," declared Flossie, who seemed bound to start a dispute. Perhaps she was so tired that she was fretful.

"Say, can't you two stop disputing all the while?" asked Bert, in a low voice. "You make papa and mamma nervous."

"Well, an elephant is big, anyhow," said Freddie.

"So he is, little Fat Fireman," said Nan, "Come and sit with me, and we can see the men catch the monkeys."

The work of getting the escaped animals back into their cages was going on rapidly. Some of the passengers went out to watch, but the Bobbseys stayed in their seats, Mr. Bobbsey thinking this best. The catching of the monkeys was the hardest work, but soon even this was accomplished.

The wait seemed very tiresome when there was nothing more to watch, and Mr. Bobbsey looked about for some railroad man of whom he could inquire how much longer delay there would be. The conductor came through the car.

"When will we start?" asked Mr. Bobbsey.

"Not for some time, I'm afraid," spoke the tickettaker. "The wreck is a worse one than I thought at first, and some of the cars of the circus train are across the track so we can't get by. We may be here two hours yet."

"That's too bad. Where are we?"

"Just outside of Whitewood."

"Oh, that's near home!" exclaimed Mrs. Bobbsey. "Why can't we get out, Richard, walk across the fields to the trolley line, and take that home? It won't be far, and we'll be there ever so much quicker."

"Well, we could do that, I suppose," said her husband, slowly.

"That's what a number of passengers did," said the conductor. "There's no danger in going out now—all the animals are back in their cages."

"Then that's what we'll do, children," said their father. "Gather up your things, and we'll take the trolley home. The moon is coming up, and it will soon be light."

"I'm hungry," said Freddie, fretfully.

"So am I," added his twin sister.

"Well, I have some crackers and cookies in my bag," replied Mrs. Bobbsey. "You can eat those on the way. Nan, go tell Dinah that we're going to take a trolley. We can each carry something."

"I'll carry Snoop," exclaimed Freddie. He hurried down the aisle to where the cook was now standing, intending to get the box containing his pet cat.

"Where's Snoop, Dinah?" he asked.

"Heah he am!" she said, lifting up the slatbox. "He ain't made a sound in all dis confusion, nuther."

The next moment Freddie gave a cry of dismay:

"Snoop's gone!" he wailed. "He broke open the box and he's gone! Oh, where is Snoop?"

"Ma sakes alive!" cried Dinah. The box was empty!

A hurried search of the car did not bring forth the black pet. Mr. and Mrs. Bobbsey, and some of the passengers, joined in the hunt. But there was no Snoop, and a slat that had pulled loose from one side of the box showed how he had gotten out.

"Most likely Snoop got frightened when the train stopped so suddenly, and broke loose," said Mr. Bobbsey. "We may find him outside."

"I—I hope an elephant didn't step on him," said Flossie, with a catch in her breath.

"Ohooo! Maybe a tiger or a lion has him!" wailed Freddie. "Oh, Snoop!"

"Be quiet, dear, we'll find him for you," said Mrs. Bobbsey, as she opened her satchel to get out some cookies. Then she remembered something.

"Freddie, where is that silver cup?" she asked. "You had it to get a drink. Did you give it back to me?"

"No, mamma, I—I"

"He gave the fat lady a drink from it," spoke Flossie, "and she didn't give it back."

"The train stopped just as she was drinking," went on Freddie. "I sat down on the floor—hard, and I saw the water spill on her. The fat lady has our silver cup! Oh, dear!"

"And she's gone—and Snoop is gone!" cried Flossie. "Oh! oh!"

"Is that so—did you let her take your cup, Freddie?" asked his papa.

Freddie only nodded. He could not speak.

"That fat lady was with the circus," said one of the men passengers. "Maybe you can see her outside."

"I'll look," said Mr. Bobbsey, quickly. "That cup is too valuable to lose. Come, children, we'll see if we can't find Snoop also, and then we'll take a trolley car for home."

A Queer Dog

Papa Bobbsey first looked for some of the circus men of whom he might inquire about the fat lady. There was much confusion, for a circus wreck is about as bad a kind as can happen, and for some time Mr. Bobbsey could find no one who could tell him what he wanted to know.

Meanwhile Mrs. Bobbsey kept the four children and Dinah with her, surrounding their little pile of baggage off to one side of The tracks.

Some of the big torches were still burning, and the full moon was coming up, so that there was plenty of light, even if it was night.

"Oh, but if we could only find Snoop!" cried Freddie. "Here, Snoop! Snoop!" he called.

"I had much rather find the fat lady, and get back your lovely silver cup," said Mrs. Bobbsey. "I hope she hasn't taken it away with her."

"She had it in her hand when the train, stopped with such a jerk," explained Flossie. "Oh, but mamma, don't you want us to find Snoop—dear Snoop?"

"Of course I do. But I want that silver cup very much, too. I hope your father finds it."

"But there never could be another Snoop," cried Flossie. "Could there, Freddie? And we could get another silver cup."

"Don't be silly," advised Bert, rather shortly.

"Oh, don't talk that way to them," said Nan. "They do love that cat so. Never mind, Flossie and Freddie. I'm sure we'll find him soon. Here comes papa."

Mr. Bobbsey came back, looking somewhat worried.

"Did you find her?" asked Mrs. Bobbsey anxiously.

"No," he replied, with a shake of his head. "She was the circus fat lady all right. It seems she missed the showtrain, and came on in ours. And, when we stopped she got out, and went up ahead. Part of the circus train, carrying the performers, was not damaged and that has gone on. The fat lady is with that, so one of the men said."

"And, very likely, she has carried off our silver cup," exclaimed Mrs. Bobbsey. "Oh dear! Can you find her later, Richard?"

"I think so. But it will take some time. The circus is going to Danville—that's a hundred miles from here. But I will write to the managers there, and ask them to get our cup from the fat lady."

"But where is Snoop?" asked Freddie, with much anxiety.

"I don't know, my dear," answered Mr. Bobbsey. "I asked the circus men if they had seen him, but they were too busy to remember. He may be running around some where. But we can't wait any longer. We must get home. I'll speak to one of the switchmen, who stay around here, and if they see Snoop I'll have them keep him for us. We'll come back tomorrow and inquire."

"But we want Snoop now!" exclaimed Freddie, fretfully.

"I'm afraid we can't get him," said Mrs. Bobbsey, gently. "Come, children, let's go home now, and leave it to papa. Oh, to think of your lovely silver cup being gone!"

"Snoop is worse," said Flossie, almost crying.

"I—I'm sorry I let the fat lady take the cup," spoke Freddie.

"Oh, you meant all right, my dear," said his mamma, "and it was very kind of you. But we really ought to start. We may miss a trolley. Come, Dinah, can you carry all you have?"

"'Deed an' I can, Mrs. Bobbsey. But I suah am sorry 'bout dat ar' Snoop."

"Oh, it wasn't your fault, Dinah," said Nan quickly. "He is getting to be such a big cat that he can easily push the slats off his box, now. We must make it stronger next time."

Flossie and Freddie wondered if there would be a "next time," for they feared Snoop was gone forever. They did not worry so much about the silver cup, valuable as it was.

With everyone in the little party carrying something, the Bobbsey family set off across, the fields toward the distant trolley line that would take them nearly home. The moon was well up now, and there was a good path across the fields. Nan and Bert were talking about the wreck, and recalling some of the funny incidents of catching the circus animals.

Flossie and Freddie were wondering whether they would ever see their pet cat again. They had had him so long that he seemed like one of the family.

"Maybe he ran off and joined the circus," said Flossie.

"Maybe," spoke her brother. "But he can't do any tricks, so they won't want him in a show."

"He can so do tricks! He can chase his tail and almost grab it."

"That isn't a trick."

"It is so—as much as standing on your head."

"Children—children—I don't know what I'll do with you if you don't stop that constant bickering," said Mrs. Bobbsey. "You must not dispute so."

"Well, mamma, but isn't chasing your tail a trick?" asked Flossie. "Freddie says it isn't."

"Well, it isn't a circus trick, anyhow," declared her brother. "I meant a circus trick."

"Well, Snoop is a good cat, anyhow," went on Flossie, "and I wish we had him back."

"Oh, so do I!" exclaimed Freddie, and thus that little dispute ended.

They were walking along through a little patch of woods now, when Bert, who was the last one in line, suddenly called out:

"Something is coming after us!"

"Coming after us? What do you mean?" asked Nan quickly, as she hurried to her father's side.

"I mean I've been listening for two or three minutes now, to some animal following after us along the path. Some big animal, too."

Flossie and Freddie both ran back and took hold of their mother's hands.

"Don't scare the children, Bert," said Mr. Bobbsey, a bit sternly. "Did you really hear something?"

"Yes, father. It's some animal walking behind us. Listen and you can hear it your self."

They all listened. It was very quiet. Then from down the hard dirt path they all heard the "pitpat, pitpat" of the footsteps of some animal. It was coming on slowly.

For a moment Mr. Bobbsey thought of the wild animals of the circus. In spite of what the men had said perhaps one of the beasts might have escaped from its cage. The others in the little party evidently thought the same thing. Mrs. Bobbsey drew her children more closely about her.

"'Deed an' if it's one ob dem elephants," said Dinah, "an' if he comes fo' me I'll jab mah hat pin in his long nose—dat's what I will!"

"It can't be an elephant," said Mr. Bobbsey. "One of the big beasts would make more noise than that. It may be one of the monkeys—I don't see how they could catch them all—they were so lively and full of mischief."

"Oh, if it's a monkey, may we keep it?" begged Flossie. "I just love a monkey."

"Mercy, child! What would we do with it around the house?" cried Mrs. Bobbsey. "Richard, can you see what it is?"

Mr. Bobbsey peered down the road.

"I can see something," he said. "It's coming nearer."

"Oh dear!" cried Nan, trembling with fear.

Just then a bark sounded—a friendly bark.

"It's a dog!" said Mrs. Bobbsey. "Oh, I'm so glad it wasn't an elephant," and she hugged Freddie and Flossie.

"Pooh! I wasn't afraid!" cried Freddie. "If it had been an elephant I—I'd give him a cookie, and maybe he'd let me ride home on his back."

The animal barked louder now, and a moment later he came into sight on a moonlit part of the path. The children could see that it was a big, shaggy white dog, who wagged his tail in greeting as he walked up to them.

"Oh, what a lovely dog!" cried Nan. "I wonder where he belongs?"

The fine animal came on. Bert snapped his fingers, boy-fashion.

Instantly the dog stood up on his hind legs and began marching about in a circle on the path.

"Oh, what a queer dog!" cried Flossie. "Oh I wish he was ours!"

Home in an Auto

Down on his four legs dropped the big white dog, and with another wag of his fluffy tail he came straight for Flossie.

"Be careful!" warned Mamma Bobbsey.

"He won't hurt her!" declared Bert. "That's a good dog, anyone can tell that. Here, doggie; come here!" he called.

But the dog still advanced toward Flossie, who shrank back a bit timidly.

"You never can tell what dogs will do," said Mrs. Bobbsey. "It is best to be careful."

"I guess he knew what Flossie said to him," spoke up Freddie. "He knows we like dogs."

The dog barked a little, and, coming up to where Flossie was, again stood on his hind legs.

"That's a queer trick," said Mr. Bobbsey. "I guess this dog has been trained. He probably belongs around here."

"I wish he belonged to us," sighed Nan. Like Flossie and Freddie she, too, loved animals.

"Maybe we can keep him if we don't find Snoop?" suggested Freddie. "Oh, papa, will you get Snoop back?" and Freddie's voice sounded as though he was going to cry.

"Yes, yes, of course I will," said Mr. Bobbsey quickly. He did not want the children to fret now, with still quite a distance yet to go home, and that in a trolley car. There were bundles to carry, weary children to look after, and Mrs. Bobbsey was rather tired also. No wonder Papa Bobbsey thought he had many things to do that night.

"Come along, children," called Mrs. Bobbsey, "it is getting late, and we are only about half way to the trolley. Oh dear! If that circus had to be wrecked I wish it could have waited until our train passed."

"Are you very tired?" asked her husband. "I can take that valise."

"Indeed you'll not. You have enough."

"Lemme have it, Massa Bobbsey," pleaded Dinah. "I ain't carryin' half enough. I's pow'ful strong, I is."

"Nonsense, Dinah!" said Mr. Bobbsey. "I can manage, and your arms are full."

"I—I wish she had Snoop," said Freddie, but he was so interested in watching the queer dog that he half forgot his sorrow over the lost cat.

The dog seemed to have made great friends with Flossie. She was patting him on the head now, for the animal, after marching about on his hind legs, was down on all fours again.

"Oh, mamma, he's awful nice!" exclaimed Flossie. "He's just as gentle, and he's soft, like the little toy lamb I used to have."

"Indeed he does seem to be a gentle dog," said Mrs. Bobbsey. "But come along now. Don't pet him any more, or he may follow us. Flossie, and whoever owns him would not like it. Come on."

"Forward—march!" called Freddie, strutting along the moonlit path as much like a soldier as he could imitate, tired as he was.

The Bobbseys and their faithful Dinah started off again toward the distant trolley that would take them to their home. The dog sat down and looked after them.

"I—I wish he was ours," said Flossie wistfully, waving her hand to the dog.

The Bobbseys had not gone on very far before Nan, looking back, called out:

"Oh, papa, that dog is following us!"

"He is?" exclaimed Mr. Bobbsey. "That's queer. He must have taken a sudden liking to us. But I guess he'll go back where he belongs pretty soon. Are you getting tired, little Fat Fireman? And you, my Fat Fairy?"

"Oh, no, papa," laughed Flossie. "I sat down so much in the train that I'm glad to stand up now."

"So am I," said Freddie, who made up his mind that he would not say he was tired if his little sister did not. And yet, truth to tell, the little Fat Fireman was very weary.

On and on went the Bobbsey family, and soon Bert happened to look back, and gave a whistle of surprise.

"That dog isn't going home, papa," he said. "He's still after us, and look! now he's running."

They all glanced back on hearing this. Surely enough the big white dog was running after them, wagging his tail joyfully, and barking from time to time.

"This will never do!" exclaimed Mr. Bobbsey. "Whoever owns him may think we are trying to take him away. I'll drive him back. Go home! Go back, sir!" exclaimed Papa Bobbsey in stern tones.

The dog stopped wagging his tail. Then he sat down on the path, and calmly waited. Mr. Bobbsey walked toward him.

"Oh, don't—don't whip him, papa!" exclaimed Flossie.

"I don't intend to," said Mr. Bobbsey. "But I must be stern with him or he will think I'm only playing. Go back!" he cried.

The dog stretched out on the path, his head down between his fore paws.

"He—he looks—sad," said Freddie. "Maybe he hasn't any home, papa."

"Oh, of course a valuable dog like that has a home," declared Bert.

"But maybe they didn't treat him kindly, and he is looking for a new one," suggested Nan, hopefully.

"He doesn't seem illtreated," spoke Mrs. Bobbsey. "Oh, I do wish he'd go back, so we could go on."

Mr. Bobbsey pretended to pick up a stone and throw it at the dog, as masters sometimes do when they do not want their dogs to follow them. This dog only wagged his tail, as though he thought it the best joke he had ever known.

"Go back! Go back, I say!" cried Papa Bobbsey in a loud voice. The dog did not move.

"I guess he won't follow us any more," went on Mr. Bobbsey. "Hurry along now, children. We are almost at the trolley." He turned away from the dog, who seemed to be asleep now, and the family went on. For a minute or two, as Nan could tell by looking back, the dog did not follow, but just as the Bobbseys were about to make a turn in the path, up jumped the animal and came trotting on after the children and their parents, wagging his tail so fast that it seemed as if it would come loose.

"Is he coming?" asked Flossie.

"He certainly is," answered Bert, who was in the rear. "I guess he wants us to take him home with us."

"Oh, let's do it!" begged Flossie.

"Please, papa," pleaded Freddie. "We haven't got Snoop now, so let us have a dog. And I'm sure we could teach him to do tricks—he's so smart."

"And so he's coming after us still!" exclaimed Mr. Bobbsey. "Well, well, I don't know what to do," and he came to a stop on the path.

"Couldn't we take him home just for tonight?" asked Nan, "and then in the morning we could find out who owns him and return him."

"Oh, please do," begged Freddie and Flossie, impulsively.

"But how can we take him on a trolley car?" asked Mr. Bobbsey. "The conductor would not let us."

"Maybe he would—if he was a kind man," suggested Freddie. "We could tell him how it was, and how we lost our cat."

"And our silver cup," added Flossie.

"Well, certainly the dog doesn't seem to want to go home," said Mr. Bobbsey, after he had tried two or three times more to drive the animal back. But it would not go.

"Go on a little farther," suggested Mrs. Bobbsey. "By the time we get to the trolley he may get tired, and go back. And if we want to lose him I think we can, by getting on the car quickly."

"But we don't want to lose him!" cried Freddie.

"No, no!" said Flossie. "We want to keep him. He can run along behind the trolley car. I'll ask the motorman to go slow, papa."

"My! This has been a mixedup day!" sighed Mr. Bobbsey. "I really don't know what to do."

The dog seemed to think that he was one of the family, now. He came up to Flossie and Freddie and let them pat him. His tail kept wagging all the while.

"Well, we'll see what happens where we get to the trolley," decided Mr. Bobbsey, thinking that there would be the best and only place to get rid of the dog. "Come along, children."

Freddie and Flossie came on, the dog between them, and this seemed to suit the fine animal. He had found friends, now, he evidently thought. Mr. Bobbsey wondered why so valuable a dog would leave its home. And he was very much puzzled as to what he should do if the children insisted on keeping the animal, and if it came aboard the trolley car.

"There's the car!" exclaimed Bert, as they went around another turn in the path and came to a road. Down it could be seen the headlight of an approaching trolley, and also the twin lamps of an oncoming automobile.

"Look out for the auto, children!" cried Mrs. Bobbsey.

They stood at the side of the road, and as the auto came up the man in it slowed down his machine. It was a big car and he was alone in it.

"Well, I declare!" exclaimed the autoist, as his engine stopped. "If it isn't the Bobbsey family—twins and all! What are you doing here, Mr. Bobbsey?"

"Why, it's Mr. Blake!" exclaimed Mr. Bobbsey, seeing that the autoist was a neighbor, and a business friend of his. "Oh, our train was held back by a circus wreck, so we walked across the lots to the car. We're homeward bound from the seashore."

"Well, well! A circus wreck, eh? Where did you get the dog?"

"Oh, he followed us," said Mrs. Bobbsey.

"And we're going to keep him, too!" exclaimed Flossie.

"And take him in the trolley with us," added her little brother.

"Well, well!" exclaimed Mr. Blake. "Say, now, I have a better plan than that," he went on. "Why should you folks go home in a trolley, when I have this big empty auto here? Pile in, all of you, and I'll get you there in a jiffy. Come, Dinah, I see you, too."

"Yes, sah, Massa Blake, I'se heah! Can't lose ole Dinah!"

"But we lost our cat, Snoop!" said Flossie regretfully.

"And we nearly ran over an elephant," added Freddie, bound that his sister should not tell all the news.

"Well, get in the auto," invited Mr. Blake.

"Do you really mean it?" asked Mr. Bobbsey. "Perhaps we are keeping you from going somewhere."

"Indeed not. Pile in, and you'll soon be home."

"Can we bring the dog, too?" asked Flossie.

"Yes, there's plenty of room for the dog," laughed Mr. Blake. "Lift him in."

But the strange dog did not need lifting. He sprang into the tonneau of the auto as soon as the door was opened. Mr. and Mrs. Bobbsey lifted in Flossie and Freddie, and Nan and Bert followed. Then in got Papa and Mamma Bobbsey and Mr. Blake started off.

"This is lovely," said Mrs. Bobbsey with a sigh of relief. She was more tired than she had thought.

"It certainly is kind of you, Mr. Blake," said Papa Bobbsey.

"I'm only too glad I happened to meet you. Are you children comfortable?"

"Yep!" chorused Freddie and Flossie.

"And the dog?"

"We're holding him so he won't fall out," explained Flossie. She and her little brother had the dog between them.

On went the auto, and with the telling of the adventures of the day the journey seemed very short. Soon the Bobbsey home was reached. There were lights in it, for Sam, the colored man, had been telephoned to, to have the place opened for the family. Sam came out on the stoop to greet them and his wife Dinah.

"Here we are!" cried Papa Bobbsey. "Come, Flossie Freddie we're home."

Flossie and Freddie did not answer. They were fast asleep, their heads on the shaggy back of the big dog.

Snap Does Tricks

"We'll have to carry them in," said Mr. Bobbsey, as he looked in the rear of the auto, and saw his two little twins fast asleep on the dog's back.

"I'll take 'em," said Sam kindly. "Many a time I'se carried 'em in offen de porch when dey falled asleep. I'll carry 'em in."

And he did, first taking Flossie, and then Freddie. Then he and Dinah brought in the bundles and valises, while Nan and Bert and Mr. and Mrs. Bobbsey followed, having bidden goodnight to Mr. Blake, and thanking him for the ride.

"Where—where are we?" asked Flossie, rubbing her eyes and looking around the room which she had not seen in some months.

"An'—an' where's our dog?" demanded Freddie.

"Oh, bless your hearts—that dog!" cried Mamma Bobbsey. "Sam took him out in the barn. You may see him in the morning, if he doesn't run away in the night."

The twins looked worried over this suggestion, until Sam said:

"Oh, I locked him up good an' proper in a box stall; 'deed an' I did, Mrs. Bobbsey. He won't get away tonight."

"That's—good," murmured Freddie, and then he fell asleep again.

Soon the little twins were undressed and put to bed; Nan and Bert soon followed, but Mr. and Mrs. Bobbsey stayed up a little later to talk over certain matters.

"It's good to be home again," said Mr. Bobbsey, as he looked about the rooms of the town house.

"Yes, but we had a delightful summer," spoke his wife, "and the children are so well. The country was delightful, and so was the seashore. But I think I, too, am glad to be back. It will be quite a task, though, to get the children ready for school. Flossie and Freddie will go regularly now, I suppose, and with Nan and Bert in a higher class, it means plenty of work."

"I suppose so," said her husband.

"But Dinah is a great help," went on Mrs. Bobbsey, for she did not mean to complain. Flossie and Freddie had tried a few days in the kindergarten class at school, but Flossie said she did not like it, and, as Freddie would not go without her, their parents had taken them both out in the Spring.

"There will be plenty of time to start them in the Fall," said Mrs. Bobbsey, and so it had been arranged. And now the four twins were all to attend the same school, which would open in about a week.

Flossie and Freddie were both up early the next morning, and, scarcely halfdressed, they hurried out to the barn.

"Whar yo' chillers gwine?" demanded Dinah, as she prepared to get breakfast.

"Out to see our dog," answered Freddie. "Is Sam around?"

"Yes, he's out dere somewheres, washin' de carriage. But don't yo' let dat dog bite yo'."

"We won't," said Freddie.

"He wouldn't bite anyhow," declared Flossie.

Sam opened the box stall for them, and out bounced the big white dog, barking in delight, and almost knocking down the twins, so glad was he to see them.

"What shall we call him?" asked Freddie. "Maybe we'd better name him Snoop, like our cat. I guess Snoop is gone forever."

"No, we mustn't call him Snoop," said Flossie, "for some day our cat might come back, and he'd want his own name again. We'll call our dog Snap, 'cause see how bright his eyes snap. Then if our cat comes back we'll have Snoop and Snap."

"That's a good name," decided Freddie, after thinking it over. "Snoop and Snap. I wonder how we can make this dog stand on his hind legs like he did before?"

"Bert snapped his fingers and he did it," suggested Flossie. "But maybe he'll do it now if you just ask him to."

Freddie tried to snap his fingers, but they were too short and fat. Then he patted the dog an the head and said:

"Stand up!"

At once the dog, with a bark, did so. He sat up on his hind legs and then walked around. Both the children laughed.

"I wonder if he can do any other tricks?" asked Flossie.

"I'm going to try," said her brother. "What trick do you want him to do?"

"Make him lie down and roll over."

"All right," spoke Freddie. "Now, Snap, lie down and roll over!" he called. At once the fine animal did so, and then sprang up with a bark, and a wag of his tail, as much as to ask:

"What shall I do next?"

"Oh, isn't he a fine dog!" cried Flossie. "I wonder who taught him those tricks?"

"Let's see if he can do any more," said Freddie. "There's a barrel hoop over there. Maybe he'll jump through it if we hold it up."

"Oh, let's do it!" cried Flossie, as she ran to get the hoop. Snap barked at the sight of it, and capered about as though he knew just what it was for, and was pleased at the chance to do more of his tricks. The hoop was a large one, and Freddie alone could not hold it very steady. So Flossie took hold of one side. As soon as they were in position, Freddie called:

"Come on now, Snap. Jump!"

Snap barked, ran back a little way, turned around and came racing straight for the twins. At that moment Sam Johnson came up running, a stick in his hand.

"Heah! heah!" shouted the colored man, "You let dem chillers alone, dog! Go 'way, I tells yo'!"

"That's all right, Sam," said Freddie. "Don't scare him. He's our new dog Snap, and he's going to do a trick," for the colored gardener had supposed the dog was running at Flossie and Freddie to bite them.

Snap paid no attention to Sam, but raced on. When a short distance from where Flossie and Freddie held the hoop, Snap jumped up into the air, and shot straight through the wooden circle, landing quite a way off.

"Mah gracious sakes alive!" gasped Sam. "Dat's a reg'lar circus trick—at's what it am!"

He scratched his head in surprise, and the stick he had picked up, intending to drive away the dog with, stuck straight out. In a moment Snap raced up, and jumped over the stick.

"Oh, look!" cried Flossie.

"Another trick!" exclaimed Freddie.

"Mah gracious goodness!" cried Sam. "Dat suah am wonderful!"

Snap ran about barking in delight. He seemed happy to be doing tricks.

"Let's go tell papa," said Freddie. "He'll want to know about this."

"Oh, I do hope he lets us keep him," said Flossie.

Mr. Bobbsey had not yet gone to his lumber office. He listened to what the little twins had to tell them about Snap, who lay on the lawn, seeming to listen to his own praises.

"A trick dog; eh?" exclaimed Mr. Bobbsey. "I wonder who owns him?"

"Maybe he escaped from the circus," suggested Bert, who came out just then to see how his pigeons were getting along.

"That's it!" cried Mr. Bobbsey. "I wonder I did not think of it before. The dog must have escaped from the wrecked circus train, and he followed us, not knowing what else to do. That accounts for his tricks."

"But we can keep him; can't we?" begged Flossie.

"Hum! I'll have to see about that," said Mr. Bobbsey slowly. "I suppose the circus people will want him back, for he must be valuable. Perhaps some clown trained him."

"But if we can't have Snoop, our cat, we ought to have a dog," asserted Freddie.

"I'll try to get Snoop back," said Mr. Bobbsey. "I'll have one of my men go down to the place where the wreck was, today, and inquire of the railroad men. He may be wandering about there."

"Poor Snoop!" said Nan, coming out to feed some of her pet chickens, that Sam had looked after all summer.

"And while you are about it," suggested Mrs. Bobbsey, who was on the front porch, "I wish, Richard, that you would see if you can locate that fat lady, and get back the children's silver cup."

"I will," replied Mr. Bobbsey. "I will have to write to them anyhow, about the dog, and at the same time I'll ask about the cup. Though I don't believe the fat lady meant to keep it."

"Oh, no," said Mrs. Bobbsey. "Probably she just held it, in the excitement over the wreck, and she may have left it in the car. But please write about it."

"I will," promised Mr. Bobbsey, as he started for the office, while the twins gathered about the new dog, who seemed ready to do more tricks.

Danny Rugg Is Mean

That afternoon a small fire broke out in Mr. Bobbsey's lumber yard. The alarm bell rang, and Mrs. Bobbsey, hearing it, and knowing by the number that the blaze must be near her husband's place of business, came hurrying down stairs.

"Oh, I must go and see how dangerous it is," she said to Dinah. "It is too bad to have it happen just after Mr. Bobbsey comes back from his summer vacation."

"'Deed it am!" cried the fat, colored cook. "But maybe it am only a little fire, Mrs. Bobbsey."

"I'm sure I hope so," was the answer.

As Mrs. Bobbsey was hurrying down the front walk Flossie and Freddie saw her.

"Where are you going, mamma?" they called.

"Down to papa's office," she answered. "There's a fire near his place, and—"

"Oh, a fire! Then I'm going!" cried Freddie. "Fire! Fire! Ding, dong! Turn on the water!" and he raced about quite excitedly.

"Oh, I don't know," said Mrs. Bobbsey, in doubt. "Where are Nan and Bert?" she asked.

"They went down to the lake," said Flossie. "Oh, mamma, do take us to the fire with you. We'll bring Snap along."

"Sure," said Freddie. "Hi, Snap!" he called.

The trick dog came rushing from the stable, barking and wagging his tail.

"Well, I suppose I might as well take you," said Mrs. Bobbsey. "But you must stay near me. We'll leave Snap home, though."

"Oh, no!" cried Freddie.

"He might get lost," said Mrs. Bobbsey.

That was enough for Freddie. He did not want the new pet to get lost, so he did not make a fuss when Sam came hurrying up to lock Snap in the stable. Poor Snap howled, for he wanted very much to go with the children.

The fire was, as I have said, a small one, in part of the planing mill. But the engines puffed away, and spurted water, and this pleased Freddie. Flossie stayed close to her mother, and Mrs. Bobbsey, once she found out that the main lumber yard was not in danger, was ready to come back home. But Freddie wanted to stay until the fire was wholly out.

Mr. Bobbsey came from his office to give some directions to the firemen, and saw his wife and the two twins. Then he took charge of them, and led them as close to the blaze as was safe.

"It will soon be out," he said. "It was only some sawdust that got on fire."

"I wish I could squirt some water!" sighed Freddie.

"What's that? Do you want to be a fireman?" asked one of the men in a rubber coat and a big helmet. He smiled at Mr. Bobbsey, whom he knew quite well.

"Yes, I do," said Freddie.

"Then come with me, and I'll let you help hold the hose," said the fireman. "I'll look after him," he went on, to Mrs. Bobbsey, and she nodded to show that Freddie could go.

What a good time the little fellow had, standing beside a real fireman, and helping throw real water on a real fire! Freddie never forgot that. Of course the fire was almost out, and it was only one of the small hose lines that the fireman let the little fellow help hold, but, for all that, Freddie was very happy.

"Did you write to the circus people today about our silver cup, and that trick dog?" asked Mrs. Bobbsey of her husband, that night.

"I declare, I didn't!" he exclaimed. "The fire upset me so that it slipped my mind. I'll do it the first thing tomorrow. There is no special hurry. How is the dog, by the way?"

"Oh, he's just lovely!" cried Flossie.

"And I do hope we can keep him forever!" exclaimed Freddie. "'Specially since Snoop is gone."

"Did you hear anything about our cat?" asked Nan, of her father.

"No. I sent a man to the railroad company, but no stray cat had been found. I am afraid Snoop is lost, children."

"Oh dear!" cried Flossie.

The next day, having learned from the railroad company where the circus had gone after the wreck, Mr. Bobbsey sent a letter to the manager, explaining about the lost silver cup, and the found circus dog. He asked that the fat lady be requested to write to him, to let him know if she had taken the cup by accident, and Mr. Bobbsey also wanted to know if the circus had lost a trick dog.

"There!" he exclaimed as he sent the letter to be mailed, "now we'll just have to wait for an answer."

Nan and Bert, and Flossie and Freddie were soon having almost as much fun as they had had at the seashore and in the country. Their town

playmates, who had come back from their vacations, called at the Bobbsey home, and made up games and all sorts of sports.

"For," said Grace Lavine, with whom Nan sometimes played, "school will soon begin, and we want to have all the fun we can until then."

"Let's jump rope," proposed Nan.

"All right," agreed Grace. "Here comes Nellie Parks, and we'll see who can jump the most."

"No, you mustn't do that," said Nan. "Don't you remember how you once tried to jump a hundred, and you fainted?"

"Indeed I do," said Grace. "I'm not going to be so silly as to try that again. We'll only jump a little."

Soon Nan and her chums were having good time in the yard.

Charley Mason, with whom Bert sometimes played, came over, and the two boys went for a row on the lake, in Bert's boat. Some little friends of Flossie and Freddie came over, and they had fun watching Snap do tricks.

For the circus dog, as he had come to be called, seemed to be able to do some new trick each day. He could "play dead," and "say his prayers," besides turning a back somersault. The little twins, who seemed to claim more share in Snap than did Nan and Bert, did not really know how many tricks their pet could do.

"Maybe you'll have to give him back to the circus," said Willie Flood, one of Freddie's chums.

"Well, if we do, papa may buy him, or get another dog like him," spoke Flossie.

A few days after this, when Bert was out in the front yard, watering the grass with a hose, along came Danny Rugg. Now Danny went to the same school that Bert did, but few of the boys and none of the girls, liked Danny, because he was often rough, and would hit them or want to fight, or would play mean tricks on them. Still, sometimes Danny behaved himself, and then the boys were glad to have him on their baseball nine as he was a good hitter and thrower, and he could run fast.

"Hello, Bert!" exclaimed Danny, leaning on the fence. "I hear you have a trick circus dog here."

"Who told you?" asked Bert, wondering what Danny would say next.

"Oh, Jack Parker. He says you found him."

"I didn't," spoke Bert, spraying a bed of geranium flowers. "He followed us the night of the circus wreck."

"Well, you took him all the same. I know who owns him, too; and I'm going to tell that you've got him."

"Oh, are you?" asked Bert. "Well, we think he belongs to the circus, and my father has written about it, so you needn't trouble yourself."

"He doesn't belong to any circus," went on Danny. "That dog belongs to Mr. Peterson, who lives over in Millville. He lost a trick dog, and he adverstised for it. He's going to give a reward. I'm going to tell him, and get the money."

"You can't take our dog away!" cried Freddie, coming up just then. "Don't you dare do it, Danny Rugg."

"Yes, I will!" exclaimed the mean boy, who often teased the smaller Bobbsey twins. "You won't have that dog after today."

"Don't mind him, Freddie," said Bert in a low voice. "He's trying to scare you."

"Oh, I am eh?" cried Danny. "I'll show you what I'm trying to do. I'll tell on you for keeping a dog that don't belong to you, and you'll be arrested—all of you."

Freddie looked worried, and tears came into his eyes. Bert saw this, and was angry at Danny for being so mean.

"Don't be afraid, Freddie," said Bert, "Look, I'll let you squirt the hose, and you can pretend to be a fireman."

"Oh, fine!" cried Freddie, in delight, as he took the nozzle from his older brother.

Just how it happened neither of them could tell, but the stream of water shot right at Danny Rugg, and wet him all over in a second.

"Hi there!" he cried. "Stop that! I'll pay you back for that, Fred Bobbsey," and he jumped over the fence and ran toward the little fellow.

At School

Freddie saw Danny coming, and did the most natural thing in the world. He dropped the hose and ran. And you know what a hose, with water bursting from the nozzle will sometimes do if you don't hold it just right. Well, this hose did that. It seemed to aim itself straight at Danny, and again the rough boy received a charge of water full in the face.

"Ha! ha! here! You quit that!" he gasped. "I'll fix you for that!"

The water got in his eyes and mouth, and for a moment he could not see. But with his handkerchief he soon had his eyes cleared, and then he came running toward Bert.

Danny Rugg was larger than Bert, and stronger, and, in addition, was a bullying sort of chap, almost always ready to fight some one smaller than himself.

But what Bert lacked in size and strength he made up in a bold Spirit. He was not at all afraid of Danny, even when the bully came rushing at him. Bert stood his ground manfully. He had taken up the hose where Freddie had dropped it, and the water was spurting out in a solid stream. Freddie, having gotten a safe distance away, now turned and stood looking at Danny.

Danny, too, had halted and was fairly glaring at Bert, who looked at him a bit anxiously. More than once he and the bully had come to blows, and sometimes Bert had gotten the best of it. Still he did not like a fight.

"I'll get you yet, Freddie Bobbsey!" cried Danny, shaking his fist at the little fellow. Whereupon Freddie turned and ran toward the house. Danny saw that he could not catch him in time, and so he turned to Bert.

"You put him up to do that—to douse me with water!" cried Danny angrily.

"I did not," said Bert quietly. "It was just an accident. I'm sorry."

"You are not! I say you did that on purpose or you told Freddie to, and I'm going to pay you back!"

"I tell you it was an accident," insisted Bert. "But if you want to think Freddie did it on purpose I can't stop you."

"Well, I'm going to hit you just the same," growled Danny, and he stepped toward Bert.

"You'd better look out," said Bert, with just a little smile. "There's still a lot of water in this hose," and he brought the nozzle around in front, ready to squirt on Danny if the bad boy should come too near.

Danny came to a stop.

"Don't you dare put any more water on me!" cried the bully. "If you do, I'll—" He doubled up his fists and glared at Bert.

"Then don't you come any nearer if you don't want to get wet," said Bert. "This hose might sprinkle you by accident, the same as it did when Freddie had it," he added.

"Huh! I know what kind of an accident that was!" spoke Danny, with a sneer.

"You'd better get out of the way," went on Bert quietly. "I want to sprinkle that flower bed near where you are, and if you're there you might get wet, and it wouldn't my fault."

"I'll fix you!" growled Danny, springing forward. Bert got ready with the hose, and there might have been more trouble, except that Sam, the colored man, came out on the lawn. He saw that something out of the ordinary was going on, and breaking into a run he called out:

"Am anything de mattah, Massa Bert? Am yo' habin' trouble wif anybody?"

"Well, I guess it's all over now," said Bert, as he saw Danny turn and walk toward the gate.

"If yo' need any help, jest remembah dat I'm around," spoke Sam, with a wide grin that showed his white teeth in his black, but kindly face. "I'll be right handy by, Massa Bert, yes, I will!"

"All right," said Bert, as he went on watering the flowers.

"Huh! You needn't think I'm afraid of you!" boasted Danny, but he kept on out of the gate just the same. Sam went back to his work, of weeding the vegetable garden and Bert watered the flowers. Pretty soon Freddie came back.

"Did—did Danny do anything to you?" the little fellow wanted to know.

"No, Freddie, but the hose did something to him," said Bert.

"Oh, did it wet him again?"

"That's what it did."

"Ha! Ha!" laughed Freddie. "I wish I'd been here to see it, Bert."

"Well, why did you run?"

"Oh, I—I thought maybe—mamma might want me," answered Freddie, but Bert understood, and smiled. Then he let Freddie finish watering the flowers, after which Freddie played he was a fireman, saving houses from burning by means of the hose.

Snap, the trick dog came running out, followed by Flossie, who had just been washed and combed, her mother having put a clean dress on her.

"Oh, Freddie," said the little girl, "let's make Snap do some tricks. See if he will jump over the stream of water from the hose."

"All right," agreed her little brother. "I'll squirt the water out straight, and you stand on one side of it and call Snap over. Then he'll jump."

Flossie tried this, but at first the dog did not seem to want to do this particular trick. He played soldier, said his prayers, stood on his hind legs, and turned a somersault. But he would not jump over the water.

"Come, Snap, Snap!" called Flossie. "Jump!"

Snap raced about and barked, and seemed to be having all sorts of fun, but jump he would not until he got ready. Then, when he did Freddie accidentally lowered the nozzle and Snap was soaked.

But the dog did not mind the water in the least. In fact he seemed to like it, for the day was warm, and he stood still and let Freddie wet him all over. Then Snap rolled about on the lawn, Freddie and Flossie taking turns sprinkling.

And, as might be expected, considerable water got on the two children, and when Snap shook himself, as he often did, to get some of the drops off his shaggy coat, he gave Flossie and her clean dress a regular shower bath.

Nan, coming from the house saw this. She ran up to Flossie, who had the hose just then, crying:

"Flossie Bobbsey! Oh, you'll get it when mamma sees you! She cleaned you all up and now look at yourself!"

"She can't see—there's no looking glass here," said Freddie, with a laugh.

"And you're just as bad!" cried Nan. "You'd both better go in the house right away, and stop playing with the hose."

"We're through, anyhow," said Freddie. "You ought to see Snap jump over the water."

"Oh, you children!" cried Nan, with a shake of her head. She seemed like a little mother to them at times, though she was only four years older.

Mrs. Bobbsey was very sorry to see Flossie so wet and bedraggled, and said:

"You should have known better than to play with water with a clean dress on, Flossie. Now I must punish you. You will have to stay in the house for an hour, and so will Freddie."

Poor little Bobbsey twins! But then it was not a very severe punishment, and really some was needed. It was hard when two of their little playmates came and called for them to come out. But Mrs. Bobbsey insisted on the two remaining in until the hour was at an end.

Then, when they had on dry garments, and could go out, there was no one with whom to play.

"I'm not going to squirt the hose ever again," said Freddie.

"Neither am I," said his sister. "Never, never!"

Snap didn't say anything. He lay on the porch asleep, being cooled off after his sport with the water.

"I—I wish we had our cat, Snoop, back," said Flossie. "Then we wouldn't have played in the water."

"That's so," agreed Freddie. "I wonder where he can be?"

They asked their father that night if any of the railroad men had seen their pet, but he said none had, and added:

"I'm afraid you'll have to get along without Snoop. He seems to have disappeared. But, anyhow, you have Snap."

"But some one may come along and claim him," said Freddie. "That Danny Rugg says he belongs to Mr. Peterson in Millville, father," said Bert.

"Well, I'll call Mr. Peterson up on the telephone tomorrow, and find out," spoke Mr. Bobbsey. "That much will be settled, at any rate."

"Did you hear anything from the circus people about the fat lady?" asked Mrs. Bobbsey.

"Yes, but no news," was her husband's answer. "The circus has gone to Cuba and Porto Rico for the winter, and I will have to write there. It will be some time before we can expect an answer, though, as I suppose the show will be traveling from place to place and mail down there is not like it is up here. But we may find the fat lady and the cup some day."

"And Snoop, too," put in Nan.

"Yes, Snoop too."

One fact consoled the Bobbseys in their trouble over their lost pet and cup. This was the answer received by Mr. Bobbsey from Mr. Peterson. That gentleman had lost a valuable dog, but it was a small poodle, and unlike big Snap. So far no one had claimed the trick dog, and it seemed likely that the children could keep him. They were very glad about this.

"Oh dear!" exclaimed Bert, one afternoon a few days following the fun with the hose, "school begins Monday. Only three more days of vacation!"

"I think you have had a long vacation," returned Mrs. Bobbsey, "and if Freddie and Flossie are going to do such tricks as they did the other day, with the hose, I, for one, shall be glad that you are in school."

"I like school," said Nan. "There are lot of new girls coming this term, I hear."

"Any new fellows?" asked Bert, more interested.

"I don't know. There is a new teacher in the kindergarten, though, where Flossie and Freddie will go. Nellie Parks has met her, and says she's awfully nice."

"That's good," spoke Flossie. "I like nice teachers."

"Well, I hope you and Freddie will get along well," said Mamma Bobbsey. "You are getting older you know, and you must soon begin to study hard."

"We will," they promised.

The school bell, next Monday morning, called to many rather unwilling children. The long vacation was over and class days had begun once more. The four Bobbseys went off together to the building, which was only a few blocks from their home. Mr. Tetlow was the principal, and there were half a dozen lady teachers.

"Hello, Nan," greeted Grace Lavine. "May I sit with you this term?"

"Oh, I was going to ask her," said Nellie Parks.

"Well, I was first," spoke Grace, with a pout.

"We'll be in the room where there are three seated desks," said Nan with a smile. "Maybe we three can be together."

"Oh, we'll ask teacher!" cried Nellie. "That will be lovely!"

"I'm going to sit with Freddie," declared Flossie. "We're to be together—mamma said so."

"Of course, dear," agreed Nan. "I'll speak to your teacher about it."

Bert was walking in the rear with Charley Mason, when Danny Rugg came around a corner.

"I know what I'm going to do to you after school, Bert Bobbsey!" called the bully. "You just wait and see."

"All right—I'll wait," spoke Bert quietly. "I'm not afraid."

By this time they were at the school, and it was nearly time for the last bell to ring. Danny went off to join some of his particular chums, shaking his fist at Bert as he went.

Bert Sees Something

Lessons were not very well learned that first day in school, but this is generally the case when the Fall term opens after the Summer vacation.

Just as were the Bobbsey twins, nearly all the other pupils were thinking of what good times they had had in the country, or at the seashore, and in consequence little attention was paid to reading, spelling, arithmetic and geography.

But Principal Tetlow and his teachers were prepared for this, and they were sure that, in another day or so, the boys and girls would settle down and do good work. Many of the children were in new rooms and different classes, and this did not make them feel so much "at home" as before vacation.

Nan Bobbsey's first duty, after reporting to her new teacher, was to go to the kindergarten room, and ask the teacher there if Flossie and Freddie might sit together.

"You see," Nan explained, "this is really their first real school work. They attended a few times before, but did not stay long."

"I see," spoke the pretty kindergarten instructor with a laugh, "and we must make it as pleasant for them this time as we can, so they will want to stay. Yes, my dear, Flossie and Freddie may sit together, and I'll look after them as much as I can. But, oh, there are such a lot of little tots!" and she looked about the room that seemed overflowing with small boys and girls.

Some were playing and talking, telling of their summer experiences. Others seemed frightened, and stood against the wall bashfully, little girls holding to the hands of their little brothers.

Nan looked for Freddie and Flossie. She saw her little sister trying to comfort a small girl who was almost ready to cry, while Freddie, like the manly little fellow he was, had taken charge of a small chap in whose eyes were two large tears, just ready to fall. It was his first day at school.

"Oh, I am sure your little twin brother and sister will get along all right," said the kindergarten teacher, with a smile to Nan, as she saw what Flossie and Freddie were doing. "They are too cute for anything—the little dears!"

"And they are very good," said Nan, "only of course they do—things—sometimes."

"They wouldn't be real children if they didn't," answered the teacher.

This was during a recess that had come after the classes were first formed. On her way back to her room, to see if she could arrange to sit with Grace

and Nellie at one of the new big desks, Nan saw her brother Bert. He looked a little worried, and Nan asked at once:

"What is the matter, Bert? Haven't you got a nice teacher?"

"Oh, yes, she's fine!" exclaimed Bert "There's nothing the matter at all."

"Yes there is," insisted Nan. "I can tell by your face. It's that Danny Rugg; I'm sure. Oh, Bert, is he bothering you again?"

"Well, he said he was going to."

"Then why don't you go straight and tell Mr. Tetlow? He'll make Danny behave. I'll go tell him myself!"

"Don't you dare, Nan!" cried Bert. "All the fellows would call me 'sissy,' if I let you do that. Never mind, I can look out for my self. I'm not afraid of Danny."

"Oh, Bert, I hope you don't get into fight."

"I won't, Nan—if I can help it. At least I won't hit first, but if he hits me—"

Bert looked as though he knew what he would do in that case.

"Oh dear!" cried Nan, "aren't you boys just awful!"

However, she made up her mind that if Danny got too bad she would speak to the principal about him, whether her brother wanted her to or not.

"He won't know it," thought Nan.

She had no trouble in getting permission from her teacher for herself and her two friends to sit together, and soon they had moved their books and other things to one of the long desks that had room for three pupils.

Meanwhile Flossie and Freddie got along very well in the kindergarten. At first, just as the others did, they gave very little attention to what the teacher wanted them to learn, but she was very patient, and soon all the class was gathered about the sand table, in the little low chairs, making fairy cities, caves, and even makebelieve seashore places.

"This is like the one where we were this Summer," said Flossie, as she made a hole in her sand pile to take the place of the ocean. "If I had water and a piece of wood I could show you where there was a shipwreck," she said to the girl next to her.

"That isn't the way it was," spoke Freddie, from the other side of the room. "There was more sand at the seashore than on this whole table—yes, on ten tables like this."

"There was not!" cried Flossie.

"There was too!" insisted her brother.

"Children—children!" called the teacher. "You must not argue like that—ever—in school, or out of it. Now we will sing our worksong, and after

that we will march with the flags," and she went to the piano to play. All the little ones liked this, and the dispute of Flossie and Freddie was soon forgotten.

Bert kept thinking of what might happen between himself and Danny Rugg when school was out, and when his teacher asked him what the Pilgrim Fathers did when they first came to settle in New England Bert looked up in surprise, and said:

"They fought."

"Fought!" exclaimed the teacher. "The book says they gave thanks."

"Well, I meant they fought the—er—the Indians," stammered Bert.

Poor Bert was thinking of what might take place between himself and the bully.

"Well, yes, they did fight the Indians," admitted the teacher, "but that wasn't what I was thinking of. I will ask you another question in history."

But I am not going to tire you with an account of what went on in the classrooms. There were mostly lessons there, such as you have yourselves, and I know you don't care to read about them.

Bert did not see Danny Rugg at the noon recess, when the Bobbsey twins and the other children went home for lunch. But when school was let out in the afternoon, and when Bert was talking to Charley Mason about a new way of making a kite, Danny Rugg, accompanied by several of his chums, walked up to Bert. It was in a field some distance from the school, and no houses were near.

"Now I've got you, Bert Bobbsey!" taunted Danny, as he advanced with doubledup fists. "What did you want to squirt the hose on me that time for?"

"I told you it was an accident," said Bert quietly.

"And I say you did it on purpose. I said I'd get even with you, and now I'm going to."

"I don't want to fight, Danny," said Bert quietly.

"Huh! he's afraid!" sneered Jack Westly, one of Danny's friends.

"Yes, he's a coward!" taunted Danny.

"I'm not!" cried Bert stoutly.

"Then take that!" exclaimed Danny, and he gave Bert a push that nearly knocked him down. Bert put out a hand to save himself and struck Danny, not really meaning to.

"There! He hit you back!" cried one boy.

"Yes, go on in, now, Dan, and beat him!" said another.

"Oh, I'll fix him now," boasted Danny, circling around Bert. Bert was carefully watching. He did not mean to let Danny get the best of him if he could help it, much as he did not like to fight.

Danny struck Bert on the chest, and Bert hit the bully on the cheek. Then Danny jumped forward swiftly and tried to give Bert a blow on the head. But Bert stepped to one side, and Danny slipped down to the ground.

As he did so a white box fell from his pocket. Bert knew what kind of a box it was, and what was in it, and he knew now, what had stained Danny's fingers so yellow, and what made his clothes have such a queer smell. For the box had in it cigarettes.

Danny saw where it had fallen, and picked it up quickly. Then he came running at Bert again, but a boy called:

"Look out! Here comes Mr. Tetlow, the principal!"

This was a signal for all the boys, even Bert, to run, for, though school was out, they still did not want to be caught at a fight by one of the teachers, or Mr. Tetlow.

"Anyhow, you knocked him down, Bert," said Charley Mason, as he ran on with Bert. "You beat!"

"He did not—I slipped," said Danny. "I can fight him, and I will, too, some day."

"I'm not afraid of you," answered Bert.

Mr. Tetlow did not appear to have seen the fight that amounted to so little. Perhaps he pretended not to.

Off to the Woods

Whether Danny Rugg was afraid the principal had seen him trying to force a fight on Bert, or whether the unexpected fall that came to him, caused it, no one knew, but certainly, for the next few days, Danny let Bert alone. When he passed him he scowled, or shook his fist, or muttered something about "getting even," but this was all.

Perhaps it was the thought of what Bert had seen fall from Danny's pocket that made the bully less anxious to keep up the quarrel. At any rate, Bert was left alone and he was glad of it. He was not afraid, but he liked peace.

The school days went on, and the classes settled down to their work for the long Winter term. And the thought of the snow and ice that would comparatively soon be with them, made the Bobbsey twins rejoice.

"Charley Mason and I are going to make a dandy big bob this year," said Bert one day. "It's going to carry ten fellows."

"And no girls?" asked Nan with a smile. She was walking along behind her brother, with Grace and Nellie.

"Sure, we'll let you girls ride once in a while," said Charley, as he caught up to his chum. "But you can't steer."

"I steered a bob once," said Grace, who was quite athletic for her age. "It was Danny Rugg's, too."

"Pooh! His is a little one alongside the one Charley and I are going to make!" exclaimed Bert. "Ours will be hard to steer, and it's going to have a gong on it to tell folks to get out of the way."

"That's right," agreed Charley. "And we'd better start it right away, Bert. It may soon snow."

"It doesn't feel so now," spoke Nan. "It is very warm. It feels more like ice cream cones."

"And if you'll come with me I'll treat you all to some," exclaimed Nellie Parks, whose father was quite well off. "I have some of my birthday money left."

"Oh, but there are five of us!" cried Nan, counting. "That is too much—twenty-five cents, Nellie."

"I've got fifty, and really it is very hot today."

It was warm, being the end of September, with Indian Summer near at hand.

"Well, let's go to Johnson's," suggested Nellie. "They have the best cream."

"Oh, here comes Flossie and Freddie!" exclaimed Nan. "We don't want to take them, Nellie. That means—"

"Of course I'll take them!" exclaimed Nellie, generously. "I've got fifty cents, I told you."

"I'll give them each a penny and let them run along home," offered Bert.

"No, I'm going to treat them, too," insisted Nellie. "Come on!" she called to the little twins, "we're going to get ice cream cones, it's so warm."

"Oh, goodie!" cried Flossie. "I was just wishing for one."

"So was I," added her brother.

"And I'll ask you to my party next week," the little girl went on. "I'm going to have one on my birthday."

"Oh, are you really, Flossie?" asked Nan. "I hadn't heard about it."

"Yep—I am. Mamma said I could, but she told me not to tell. I don't care, I wanted Nellie to know, as she's going to treat us to cones."

"And it's half my party, 'cause my birthday's the same day," explained Freddie. "So you can come to my party at the same time, Nellie."

"Thank you, dear, I shall. Now let's hurry to the store, for it's getting warmer all the while."

The ice cream in the funny little cones was much enjoyed by all. Bert and Charley walked on together eating, and talking of the bob sled they were going to make. They passed Danny Rugg, who looked rather enviously at them.

"Hey, Charley," called Danny, "come here, I want to speak to you."

"I'm busy now," answered Charley. "Bert and I have something to do."

"So have I. I've got a dandy plan."

"Well, I'll see you later," spoke Charley.

He had once been quite friendly with Danny, but he grew not to like his ways, and so became more chummy with Bert, who was very glad, for he liked Charley.

The two boys went on to Bert's barn, where they were going to build the bob sled. The girls, with Flossie and Freddie, went on the Bobbsey lawn, where there were some easy chairs. They sat in the shade of the trees, and Freddie had Snap do some of his tricks for the visitors.

"Can he jump through a hoop, covered with paper as they do in the circus?" asked Nellie.

"Oh, we never thought to try that," said Freddie. "I'm going to make one," and, filled with this new idea, he hurried into the house.

"Dinah," he said, "I want some paper and paste."

"Land sakes, chile! what yo' gwine t' do now?" asked the colored cook.

"Make a kite, an' take Snoop up in de air laik yo' brother Bert done once?"

"No, we're not going to do that," answered the little boy. "We're going to cover a hoop with paper, and make Snap jump through it, like in a circus."

"Mah goodness mustard pot!" cried Dinah. "What will yo' all be up to next?"

"I don't know," answered Freddie. "But will you make me some paste, Dinah? And you know we haven't got Snoop, anyhow, so we couldn't send him up on a kite tail," added Freddie.

"Deah me! Yo' chilluns done make me do de mostest wuk!" complained Dinah, but she laughed, which showed that she did not really mean it, and set at mixing some flour and water for the paste.

Flossie and Freddie insisted on making the paper covered hoop themselves. They started, but they got so much of the sticky stuff on their hands and faces that Nan feared they would soil their clothes, so she insisted on being allowed to do the pasting for them.

"But we can help, can't we?" asked Freddie.

"Yes," said Nan.

Even for Nan covering a hoop with paper was not as easy as she thought it would be. Grace and Nellie helped, but sometimes the wind would blow the paper away just as they were ready to fold it around the rim of the hoop. Then the paste would get on the girls' hands.

"What are you doing?" asked Bert, as he and Charley came from the barn. They had to stop work on their job, as they could not find a long enough plank. They decided to get one from Mr. Bobbsey's lumber yard, later.

"We're going to have Snap do the circus trick of jumping through a paper hoop," explained Nan. "Only we can't seem to get the hoop made."

"I'll do it," offered Bert, and as he and Charley had often pasted paper on their kite frames they had better luck, and soon the hoop was ready.

"Come, Snap!" called Freddie, it having been settled that he and Flossie were to hold the hoop for the dog to leap through. Snap, always ready for fun, jumped up from the grass where he had been sleeping, and frisked about, barking loudly.

"Now you hold him there, Charley," directed Bert, pointing to a spot back of where Freddie and Flossie stood. "Then I'll go over here and call him. He'll come running, and when he gets near enough, Freddie, you and Flossie hold up the paper hoop. He'll go right through it."

It worked out just as the children had planned. Snap raced away from Charley, when he heard Bert calling. He ran right between Flossie and Freddie, who raised the hoop just in time.

"Rip! Tear!" burst the paper, and Snap sailed through the hoop just as he probably had often done in the circus, perhaps from the back of a horse.

"Oh, that was fine!" cried Flossie. "Let's make another hoop!"

"Let's make a lot of 'em, and have a circus with Snap, and charge money to see him, and then we can buy a lot of ice cream for our party!" said Freddie.

"Oh, yes!" agreed his sister.

Well, they did make more hoops, and Snap seemed to enjoy jumping through them. But when Mrs. Bobbsey heard about the circus plans she decided it would make too much confusion.

"Besides, you have to help me get ready for your party," she said to the two little twins.

This took their mind off the proposed circus, but for several days after that they had much fun making hoops for Snap to jump through.

Bert and Charley got a long plank from the lumber yard, and spent much time after school in the Bobbsey barn, working over their bob sled. It was harder than they had thought it would be, and they had to call in some other boys to help them. Mr. Bobbsey, too, gave his son some advice about how to build it.

Flossie and Freddie liked it very much in school. The kindergarten teacher was very kind, and took an interest in all her pupils. "Oh, mamma!" cried Flossie, coming in one day from school, "I've learned how to make a house."

"And I can make a lantern, and a chain to hang it on, and I can put it in front of Flossie's house!" exclaimed Freddie. "And, please, mother, may I have some bread and jam. I'm awful hungry."

"Yes, dear, go ask Dinah," said Mrs. Bobbsey, with a smile. "And then you may show me how you make houses and lanterns and a chain. Are they real?"

"No," said Flossie, "they're only paper, but they look nice."

"I'm sure they must," said their mother.

After each of the twins had been given a large slice of bread and butter and jam, they showed the latest thing they had learned at school. Flossie did manage to cut out a house, that had a chimney on it, and a door, besides two windows.

Freddie took several little narrow strips of paper, and pasting the ends together, made a lot of rings. Each ring before being pasted, was slipped into

another, and soon he had A paper chain. To make the lantern he used a piece of paper made into a roll, with slits all around the middle of it where the light would have come out had there been a candle in it. And the handle was a narrow slip of paper pasted over the top of the lantern.

"Very fine Indeed," said Mamma Bobbsey. "Run out now to play. If you stay in the house too much you will soon lose all the lovely tan you got in the country, and at the seashore."

"Children," said the principal to the Bobbseys and all the others in school the next day, "I have a little treat for you. Tomorrow will be a holiday, and, as the weather is very warm, we will close the school at noon, and go off in the woods for a little picnic."

"Oh, good!" cried a number of the boys and girls, and, though it was against the rules to speak aloud during the school hours, none of the teachers objected.

"But I expect you all to have perfect marks from now until Friday," Mr. Tetlow went on. "You may bring your lunches to school with you Friday morning, if your parents will let you, and we will leave here at noon, and go to Ward's woods."

It was rather hard work to study after such good news, but, somehow, the pupils managed it. Finally Friday came, and nearly every boy and girl came to school with a basket or bundle holding his or her lunch. Mrs. Bobbsey put up two baskets for her children, Nan taking one and Bert the other.

"Oh, we'll have a lovely time!" cried Freddie, dancing about on his little fat legs.

Twelve o'clock came, and with each teacher at the head of her class, and Mr. Tetlow marching in front of all, the whole school started off for the woods.

A Scare

The way to the woods where the little school outing was to be held ran close to the road on which the Bobbsey house stood. As Freddie and Flossie, with Nan and Bert, marched along with the others, Freddie cried out:

"Oh, I hope we see mamma, and then we can wave to her."

"Yes, and maybe she'll come with us," suggested Flossie. "Wouldn't that be nice?"

"Pooh!" exclaimed Bert. "Mamma's too busy to come to a picnic today. She's expecting company."

"Yes," added Nan, "the minister and his wife are coming, and mamma's cooking a lot of things."

"Why, does a minister eat more than other folks?" asked Freddie. "If they does, I'm going to be a minister when I grow up."

"I thought you were going to be a fireman," said Bert.

"Well, I can be a fireman week days and a minister on Sundays," said the little fellow, thus solving the problem. "But do they eat so much, Nan?"

"No, of course not, only mamma wants to be polite to them, so she has a lot of things cooked up, so that if they don't like one thing they can have another. Folks always give their best to the minister."

"Then I'm surely going to be one, too," declared Flossie. "I like good things to eat. I hope our minister isn't very hungry, 'cause then there'll be some left for us when we come home from this picnic."

"Why, Flossie!" cried Nan. "We have a lovely lunch with us; plenty, I'm sure."

"Well, I'm awful hungry, Nan," said the little girl. "Besides, Sammie Jones, and his sister Julia, haven't any lunch at all. I saw them, and they looked terrible hungry. Couldn't we give them some of ours; if we have so much at home?"

"Of course we could, and it is very kind of you to think of them," said Nan, as she patted her little sister on her head. "I'll look after Sammie and Julia when we get to the grove."

In spite of what Nan and Bert had said about Mrs. Bobbsey being very busy, Flossie and Freddie looked anxiously in the direction of their house as they walked along. But no sight of their mother greeted them. They did see a friend, however, and this was none other than Snap, their new dog, who,

with many barks and wags of his fluffy tail, ran out to meet his little masters and mistresses.

"Here, Snap! Snap!" called Freddie. "Come on, old fellow!" and the dog leaped all about him.

"Let's take him to the picnic with us," suggested Flossie. "We can have lots of fun."

"And he can eat the scraps," said Nan. "Shall we, Bert?"

"I don't care. But maybe Mr. Tetlow wouldn't like it."

"You ask him, Bert," pleaded Flossie.

"Tell him Snap will do tricks to amuse us."

Bert goodnaturedly started ahead to speak to the principal, who was talking with some of the teachers, planning games for the little folk. Flossie and Freddie were patting their pet, when Danny Rugg, and one of his friends came along.

"That dog can't come to our picnic!" said Danny, with a scowl. "He might bite some of us."

"Snap never bites!" cried Freddie.

"Of course not," said Flossie.

"Well, he can't come to this picnic!" spoke Danny, angrily. "Go on home!" he cried, sharply, stooping to pick up a stone. Snap growled and showed his teeth.

"There!" cried Danny. "I told you he'd bite."

"He will not, Danny Rugg!" exclaimed Nan, who had gone up front for a minute to speak to some of the older girls. "He only growled because you acted mean to him. Now you leave him alone, or I'll tell Mr. Tetlow on you."

"Pooh! Think I care? I say no dog can come to our picnic. Go on home!" and with raised hand Danny approached Snap. Again the dog growled angrily. He was not used to being treated in this way.

"Look out, Danny Rugg," said Nan, severely, "or he may jump on you, and knock you down. He wouldn't bite you, though, mean as you are, unless I told him to do so."

"I'm not afraid of you!" cried Danny, more angry than before. "I'll get a stick and then we'll see what will happen," and he looked about for one.

"Don't let Danny beat Snap!" pleaded Flossie, tears coming into her eyes.

"I won't," said Nan, looking about anxiously for Bert. She saw him coming back, and felt better. By this time Danny had found a club, and was coming back to where Flossie, Freddie and Nan, with some of their friends, were walking along, Snap in their midst.

"I'll make that dog go home now!" cried Danny. "I'm not going to get bitten, and have hyperfobia, or whatever you call it. I'll tell Mr. Tetlow if you don't make him go home."

"Oh, don't be so smart!" exclaimed Bert, stepping out from behind a group of girls. "I've told Mr. Tetlow myself that Snap is following us, and he said to let him come along. So you needn't take the trouble, Danny Rugg. And if you try to hit our dog I'll have something more to say," and Bert stepped boldly forth.

"Huh! I'm not afraid of you," sneered Danny, but he let the club drop, and walked off with his own particular chums.

"Did Mr. Tetlow say Snap could come?" asked Freddie, anxiously.

"Yes. He said he'd be good to drive away the cows if they bothered us," answered Bert, with a smile.

After this little trouble, the Bobbseys and their friends went on toward the grove in the woods where the picnic was to be held. There was laughing and shouting, and much fun on the way, in which Snap shared.

Boys and girls would run to one side or the other of the path to gather late flowers. Some would pick up odd stones, or pine cones, and others would find curious little creeping or crawling things which they called their friends to see.

Each teacher had charge of her special class, but she did not look too closely after them, for it was a day to be happy and free from care, with no thought of school or lessons.

"We'll make Snap do some tricks when we get to the grove," said Flossie.

"Yes, we'll have a little circus," added her brother.

"Can he stand on his head?" one girl wanted to know.

"Well, he can turn a somersault, and he's on his head for a second while he's doing that," explained Freddie, proudly.

"Can he roll over and over?" a boy wanted to know. "We had a dog, once, that could."

"Snap can, too," said Flossie. "Roll over, Snap!" she ordered, and the dog, with a bark, did so. The children laughed and some clapped their hands. They thought Snap was about the best dog they had ever seen.

No accidents happened on the way to the grove, except that one little boy tried to cross a brook on some stones, instead of the plank which the others used. He slipped in and got his feet wet, but as the day was warm no one worried much.

Finally the grove was reached. It was in a wooded valley, with hills on either side, and a cold, clear spring of water at one end, where everyone could

get a drink. And that always seems to be what is most wanted at a picnic—a drink of water.

Mr. Tetlow called all the children together, before letting them go off to play, and told them at what time the start for home would be made, so that they would not be late in coming back to the meeting place.

"And now," he said, "have the best fun you can. Play anything you wish—school games if you like—but don't get too warm or excited. And don't go too far away. You may eat your luncheon when you like."

"Then let's eat ours now," suggested Flossie. "I'm awful hungry."

"So am I," said Freddie. So Nan and Bert decided that the little ones might at least have a sandwich and a piece of cake. Nor did they forget the two little Jones children, who had no lunch. The Bobbseys were well provided and soon Sammie and Julia were smiling and happy as they sat beneath a tree, eating.

Then came all sorts of games, from tag and jumping rope, to blindman's bluff and hide-and-seek. Snap was made to do a number of tricks, much to the amusement of the teachers and children. Danny Rugg, and some of the older boys, got up a small baseball game, and then Danny, with one or two chums, went off in a deeper part of the woods. Bert heard one of the boys ask another if he had any matches.

"I know what they're going to do," whispered Bert to Nan.

"What?" she asked.

"Smoke cigarettes. I saw Danny have a pack."

Nan was much shocked, but she did not see anything. She was glad Bert did not smoke.

Bert went off with some boys to see if they could catch any fish in the deeper part of the brook, about half a mile from the picnic grove, and Nan, with one or two girls about her own age, took a little walk with Flossie and Freddie to gather some late wild flowers that grew on the side of one of the hills.

They found a number of the blossoms, and were making pretty bouquets of them, when Freddie, who had gone on a little ahead of the rest, came running back so fast that he nearly rolled to the bottom of the hill, so fat and chubby was he.

"What's the matter? What is it?" asked Nan, catching her brother just in time.

"Up there!" he gasped. "It's up there! A great big black one!"

"A big black what—bug?" asked Nan, ready to laugh.

"No! a big black snake! I almost stepped on it."

"A snake! Oh, dear!" screamed the girls.

"Call Mr. Tetlow!" said Flossie. "He's got a book about snakes, and he'll know what to do."

"Come on!" cried Nellie Parks. "I'm going to run!"

"So am I!" added Grace Lavine. "Oh, it may chase us!"

In fright the children turned, Freddie looking back at the spot where he thought he had seen the snake.

Danny's Trick

Nan Bobbsey stood for a moment, she hardly knew why. Perhaps she wanted to see the big snake of which Freddie spoke. It certainly was not because she liked reptiles.

Then she thought she saw something long and black wiggling toward her, and, with a little exclamation of fright, she, too, turned to follow the others. But, as she did so, she saw their dog Snap come running up the hill, barking and wagging his tail. He seemed to have lost the children for a moment and to be telling them how glad he was that he had found them again.

Straight up the hill, toward where Freddie had said the snake was, rushed Snap.

"Here! Come back! Don't go there!" cried Nan.

"No, don't let him—he may be bitten!" added Flossie. "Come here, Snap!"

But Snap evidently did not want to mind. On up the hill he rushed, pausing now and then to dig in the earth. Nearer and nearer he came to where the little Bobbsey boy had said the snake was hiding in the grass and bushes.

"Oh, Snap! Snap!" cried Freddie. "Don't go there!" But Snap kept on, and Freddie, afraid lest his pet dog be bitten, caught up a stone and threw it at the place. His aim was pretty good, but instead of scaring away the snake, or driving back Snap, the fall of the stone only made Snap more eager to see what was there that his friends did not want him to get.

With a loud bark he rushed on, and the children, turning to look, saw something long and black, and seemingly wiggling, come toward them.

"Oh, the snake! The snake!" cried Nan.

"Run! Run!" shouted Grace.

"Come on!" exclaimed Nellie Parks, in loud tones.

"Freddie! Freddie!" called Flossie, afraid lest her little brother be bitten.

Snap rushed at the black thing so fiercely that he turned a somersault down the hill, and rolled over and over. But he did not mind this, and in an instant was up again. Once more he rushed at the black object, but the children did not watch to see what happened, for they were running away as fast as they could.

Then Freddie, anxious as to what would become of Snap if he fought a snake, looked back. He saw a strange sight. The dog had in his mouth the

long, black thing, and was running with it toward the Bobbseys and their friends.

"Oh, Nan! Nan! Look! Look!" cried Freddie. "Snap has the snake! He's bringing it to us!"

"Oh, he mustn't do that!" shouted Nan. "It may bite him or us."

"Run! Run faster!" shrieked Grace.

But even though it was down hill the children could not run as fast as Snap, and he soon caught up to them. Running on a little way ahead he dropped the black thing. But instead of wiggling or trying to bite, it was I very still.

"It—it's dead," said Nan. "Snap has killed it."

Freddie was braver now. He went closer.

"Why—why!" he exclaimed. "It isn't a snake at all! It's only an old black root of a tree, all twisted up like a snake! Look, Nan—Flossie!"

Taking courage, the girls went up to look. Snap stood over it, wagging his tail as proudly as though he had captured a real snake. As Freddie had said, it was only a tree root.

"But it did look a lot like a snake in the grass," said the little fellow.

"It must have," agreed Nan. "It looked like one even when Snap had it. But I'm glad it wasn't."

"So am I," spoke Grace, and Nellie made like remark.

Snap frisked about, barking as though to ask praise for what he had done.

"He is a good dog," observed Freddie, hearing which the animal almost wagged his tail off. "And if it had been a real snake he'd have gotten it; wouldn't you?" went on the little boy.

If barks meant anything, Snap said, with all his heart, that he certainly would—that not even a dozen snakes could frighten a big dog like him.

The children soon got over the little scare, and went back up the hill again to gather more flowers. Snap went with them this time, running about here and there.

"If there are any real snakes," said Freddie, "he'll scare them away. But I guess there aren't any."

"I hope not," said Nan, but she and the others kept a sharp lookout. However, there was no further fright for them, and soon, with their hands filled with blossoms the Bobbseys and the others went back to the main party.

Some of the teachers were arranging games with their pupils, and Nan, Flossie and Freddie joined in, having a good time. Then, when it was almost time to start for home, Mr. Tetlow blew loudly on a whistle he carried to call in the stragglers.

"Where's Bert?" asked Flossie, looking about for her older brother.

"I guess he hasn't come back from fishing yet," said Nan. "Come, Flossie and Freddie, I have a little bit of lunch left, and you might as well eat it, so you won't be hungry on the way home."

The littler Bobbsey twins were glad enough to do this. Then they had to have a drink, and Nan went with them to the spring, carrying a glass tumbler she had brought.

"This isn't like our nice silver cup that the fat lady took in the train," said Freddie, as he passed the glass of water very carefully to Flossie.

"No," she said, after she had taken her drink. "I wonder if papa will ever get that back?"

"He said, the other day," remarked Nan, as she got some water for Freddie, "that he hadn't heard from the circus yet. But I think he will. It isn't like Snoop, our cat. We don't know where he is, but we're pretty sure the fat lady has the cup."

"Poor Snoop!" cried Freddie, as he thought of the fine black cat. "Maybe some of the railroad men have him."

"Maybe," agreed Flossie.

When they got back to where the teachers and principal were, Bert and the boys who bad gone fishing had returned. They had one or two small fish.

"I'm going to have mamma cook them for my supper," said Bert, proudly holding up those he had caught.

"They're too small—there won't be anything left of them after they're cleaned," said Nan, who was quite a little housekeeper.

"Oh, yes, there will," declared her brother. "I'm going fishing again tomorrow and, catch more."

Mr. Tetlow was going about among the teachers, asking if all their pupils were on hand, ready for the march back. Danny Rugg and some of his close friends were missing.

"They ought not to have gone off so far," said Mr. Tetlow, as he blew several times on the whistle. Soon Danny and the other boy, were seen coming from a distant part of the grove. One of the boys, Harry White, looked very pale, and not at all well.

"What is the matter?" asked Mr. Tetlow, and he looked curiously at Danny and the others, and sniffed the air as though he smelled something.

"I—I guess I ate too many—apples," said Harry, in a faint voice. "We found an orchard, and—"

"I told you not to go into orchards, and take fruit," said Mr. Tetlow, severely.

"The man said we could," remarked Danny. "We asked him."

"Then you should not have eaten so many," said Mr. Tetlow. "I can't see how ripe apples, which are the only kind there are this time of year—could make you ill unless you ate too many," and he looked at Danny and Harry sharply. But they did not answer.

The march home was not as joyful as the one to the grove had been, for most of the children were tired. But they all had had a fine time, and there were many requests of the teachers to have another picnic the next week.

"Oh, we can't have them every week, my dears," said Miss Franklin, who had charge of Flossie, Freddie and some others in the kindergarten class. "Besides, it will soon be too cool to go out in the woods. In a little while we will have ice and snow, and Thanksgiving and Christmas."

"That will be better than picnics," said Freddie. "I'm going to have a new sled."

"I'm going to get a new doll, that can walk," declared Flossie, and then she and the others talked about the coming holidays.

At school several days in the following week little was talked of except the picnic, the snake scare from the old tree root, the catching of the fish, and the illness of Harry White, for that boy was quite sick by the time town was reached, and Mr. Tetlow called a carriage to send him home.

"And I can guess what made him sick too," said Bert to Nan, privately.

"What?" she asked.

"Smoking cigarettes."

"How do you know?"

"Because when I and some of the other fellows were fishing we saw Danny and his crowd smoking in the woods. They offered us some, but we wouldn't take any. Harry said he was sick then, but Danny only laughed at him."

"That Danny Rugg is a bad boy," said Nan, severely. But she was soon to see how much meaner Danny could be.

Workmen had recently finished putting some new water pipes, and a place for the children to drink, in the school yard, and one morning, speaking to the whole school, Mr. Tetlow made a little speech, warning the children not to play with the faucets, and spray the water about, as some had done, in fun.

"Whoever is caught playing with the faucets in the yard after this will be severely punished," he said.

As it happened, Flossie and Freddie were not at school that day, Freddie having a slight sore throat. His mother kept him home, and Flossie would not go without him. So they did not hear the warning, and Bert and Nan did not think to tell the smaller children of it.

Two days later Freddie was well enough to go back to class, and Flossie accompanied him. It was at the morning recess when, as Freddie went to get a drink at one of the new faucets, Danny saw him. A gleam of mischief came into the eyes of the school bully.

"Want to see the water squirt, Freddie?" asked Danny. "That's a new kind of faucet. It squirts awful far."

"Does it?" asked Freddie, innocently. "How do you make it?" He had no idea it was forbidden fun.

"Just put your thumb over the hole, and turn the water on," directed Danny. "You, too, Flossie. It won't hurt you."

Danny looked all around, thinking he was unobserved as he gave this bad advice. Naturally, Freddie and Flossie, being so young, suspected nothing. They covered the opening of the faucet with their thumbs, and turned on the water. It spurted in a fine spray, and they laughed in glee. That they wet each other did not matter.

Danny, seeing the success of his trick, walked off as he saw Mr. Tetlow coming. The Bobbsey twins were so intent on spurting the water that they did not observe the principal until he was close to them. Then they started as he called out sharply:

"Freddie! Flossie! Stop that! You know that it is forbidden! Go to my office at once and I will come and see you later. You will be punished for this!"

With tears in their eyes the little twins obeyed. They could not understand it.

The Children's Party

When Mr. Tetlow, a little later, entered his office he found Flossie and Freddie standing by one of the windows, looking out on the other children marching to their classrooms. They had cried a little, but had stopped now.

"I am very sorry to have to punish you two twins," said the principal, "but I had given strict orders that no one was to play with that water. Why did you do it?"

"Because," answered Flossie.

"Danny Rugg told us to," added Freddie. "He said it was a new kind of faucet."

"Now be careful," warned Mr. Tetlow. Often before he had heard pupils say that someone else told them to break certain rules. "Are you sure about this?" he asked.

"Yes! sir," said Freddie, eagerly. "Danny told us to do it."

"But didn't you know it was forbidden?"

"No, sir," answered Flossie.

"Why, I spoke of it in all the rooms."

"We wasn't here yesterday or the day before," said Flossie. "Freddie was sick."

Mr. Tetlow began to understand.

"I will look this up," he said, "and if find—"

He was interrupted by a boy from one of the higher classes coming in with a note from his teacher. She wanted a new box of chalk.

"When you go back, George," said the principal to the boy, as he gave him what the teacher had sent for, "go to Miss Hegan's class, and have her send Danny Rugg to me. Flossie and Freddie say he told them to spray water with one of the new faucets."

"Yes, sir, he did!" exclaimed George. "I heard him, but I didn't think they would do it. He did tell them."

At this unexpected information Mr. Tetlow was much surprised.

"If that is the case, Danny is the one to be punished," he said. "I am sorry, Flossie and Freddie, that I suspected you. You may go back to your class, and I will write your teacher a note, saying you may go out half an hour ahead of the others to make up for coming to my office. But, after this, no matter whether anyone tells you or not, don't spray the water."

"No, sir, we won't!" exclaimed the Bobbsey twins, now happy again.

Danny Rugg was punished by being kept in after school for several days, and Mr. Tetlow sent home a note to his father, explaining what a mean trick the bully had played.

"I wish I had heard Danny telling you that—just to get you in trouble," said Bert, when he was told of what had happened. "I'd have fixed him."

"Oh, don't get into any more fights," begged Nan.

Bert did not come to blows with Danny over this latest trouble, but he did tell the bully, very plainly, what he thought of him, and said if Danny ever did a thing like that again that he would not get off so easily.

"Oh, I'm not afraid of you," sneered Danny.

Lessons and fun made up many school days for the Bobbsey twins. And, as the Fall went on, lessons grew a little harder. Even Freddie and Flossie, young as they were, had little tasks to do that kept them busy. But they liked their school and the teacher, and many were the queer stories they brought home of the happenings in the classroom.

It was now toward the end of October, and the weather was getting cooler, though during the day it was still very warm at times. The twins, as did their friends, looked forward to the coming of Winter and the Christmas holidays.

Thanksgiving, too, would be a time of rejoicing and of good things to eat, and this occasion was to be made more of than usual this time, for some boys and girls the Bobbseys had met in the country and at the seashore were to be invited to spend a few days in Lakeport.

But before this there was another event down on the program. This was to be a party for Flossie and Freddie, the occasion being their joint birthdays.

"And we're going to have candy!" cried Freddie, when the arrangements were talked over.

"And ice cream"—added Flossie—"a whole freezer full; aren't we, mamma?"

"Well, I guess a small freezer full won't be any too much," said Mrs. Bobbsey, smiling. "But I hope none of you eat enough to make yourselves ill."

"We won't," promised Freddie and Flossie.

There were busy times in the home of the twins the next few days, for though Nan and Bert's birthdays were not to be observed, still they were to have their part in the jolly celebration.

Invitations were sent out, on little sheets of note paper, adorned with flowers, and in cute little envelopes. Flossie and Freddie took them to the post-office themselves.

"My! what a lot of mail!" exclaimed the clerk at the stamp window, as he saw the children dropping the invitations into the slot. "Uncle Sam will have to get some extra men to carry that around, I guess. What's it all about?"

"We're going to have a party," said Flossie, proudly.

Just then Danny Rugg came into the post-office.

"A party; eh?" he sneered. "I'm coming to it, I am; and I'm going to have two plates of ice cream."

"You are not!" cried Freddie. "My mamma wouldn't let a boy like you come to our party."

"'Specially not after what you did—telling us to play in the water," added Freddie. "You can't come!"

"Yes, I can," insisted Danny, just to tease the children.

For a moment Flossie and Freddie almost believed him, he seemed so much in earnest about it.

"You can't come you haven't any invitation," said Flossie, suddenly.

"I'll take one of those you put in the box," went on the mean boy.

"He won't dare—will he?" and Freddie appealed to the mail clerk.

"I should say not!" said the man at the stamp window. "If he does Uncle Sam will be after him."

"Well, I'm coming to that party all the same!" insisted Danny, with a grin on his freckled face.

Flossie and Freddie were so worried about him that they told their mother, but she assured them that Danny would not come to spoil their fun.

Finally the afternoon and evening of the party arrived, for the little folks were to come just before supper, play some games, eat, and then stay until about nine o'clock.

Flossie and Freddie had been dressed in their prettiest clothes, and Nan and Bert also attired for the affair. The ice cream had come from the store, all packed in ice and salt, and Dinah had set it out on the back stoop, where it would be cooler.

Dinah was very busy that day. She hurried about here and there, helping Mrs. Bobbsey. Sam, her husband, also had plenty to do.

"I 'clar t' gracious goodness!" Dinah exclaimed, "I suah will get thin ef dish yeah keeps up! I ain't set down a minute dis blessed day. My feet'll drop off soon I 'specs."

"Will they, really, Dinah?" asked Freddie. "And can we watch 'em fall?"

"Bress yo' hearts, honeys!" exclaimed the colored cook, "I didn't mean it jest dat way. But suffin's suah gwine t' happen—I feels it in mah bones!"

And something was to happen, though not exactly what Dinah expected.

Finally all was in readiness for the guests. The good things to eat were in the kitchen, all but the ice cream, which, as I have said, was out on the back porch. Flossie and Freddie had gone to the front door nearly a dozen times to see if any of the guests were in sight. Snap, as a special favor, had been allowed to stay in the house that afternoon, for the twins were going to make him do tricks for their friends.

There came a ring at the door bell.

"Here they come! Here they come!" cried Flossie.

"Let me answer, too," cried Freddie, and they both hurried through the front hall to greet the first guest at their party.

An Unpleasant Surprise

Quickly, after the first guests had arrived came the others. Nellie Parks, Grace Lavine friends of Nan, and Willie Porter and his sister Sadie, came first, and Freddie and Flossie let them in, the Porter children being some of their bestliked playmates.

All the children wore their best clothes, and for a time they were a bit stiff and unnatural, standing shyly about in corners, against the walls, or sitting on chairs.

The boys seemed to all crowd together in one part of the room, and the girls in another. Flossie and Freddie, Nan and Bert, were so busy answering the door that they did not notice this at first.

But Aunt Sarah, their mother's sister, who had come over to help Mrs. Bobbsey, looking in the parlor and library, saw what the trouble was.

"My!" she cried, with a goodnatured laugh, as she noticed how "stiff" the children were. "This will never do. You're not that way at school, I don't believe. Come, be lively. Mix up—play games. Pretend this is recess at school, and make as much noise as you like."

For a moment the boys and girls did not know what to think of this invitation. But just then Snap, the circus dog, came in the room, and, with a bark of welcome, he turned a somersault, and then marched around on his hind legs, carrying a broomstick like a gun—pretending he was a soldier. Bert had given it to him.

Then how the children laughed and clapped their hands! And Snap barked so loudly—for he liked applause that there was noise enough for even jolly Aunt Sarah. After that there was no trouble. The boys and girls talked together and soon they were playing games, and having the best kind of fun.

For some of the games simple prizes had been offered and it was quite exciting toward the end to see who would win. Flossie and Freddie thought they had never had such a good time in all their lives. Nan and Bert were enjoying themselves, too, with their friends, who were slightly older than those who had been asked for the younger Bobbsey twins.

"Going to Jerusalem," was one game that created lots of enjoyment. A number of chairs were placed in the centre of the room, and the boys and girls marched around them while Mrs. Bobbsey played the piano. But there was one less chair than there were players, so that when the music would

suddenly stop, which was a signal for each one who could, to sit down, someone was sure to be left. Then this one had to stay out of the game.

Then a chair would be taken away, so as always to have one less than the number of players, and the game went on. It was great fun, scrambling to see who would get a seat, and not be left without one, and finally there was but one chair left, while Grace Lavine and John Blake marched about. Mrs. Bobbsey kept playing quite some time, as the two went around and around that one chair. Everyone was laughing, wondering who would get a seat and so win the game, when, all at once, Mrs. Bobbsey stopped the music. She had her back turned so it would be perfectly fair.

Grace and John made a rush for the one chair, but Grace got to it first, and so she won.

"Well, I'm glad you did, anyhow," said John, politely.

Other games were "peanut races" and "potato scrambles." In the first each player had a certain number of peanuts and they had to start at one end of the room, and lay the nuts at equal distances apart across to the other side, coming back each time to their pile of peanuts to get one.

Sometimes a boy would slip, he was in such a hurry, or a girl would drop her peanuts, and this made fun and confusion.

Nan won this race easily.

In the potato scramble several rows of potatoes were made across the room. Each player was given a large spoon, and whoever first took up all his or her potatoes in the spoons one at a time, and piled them up at the far end of the room, won the game. In this Charley Mason was successful, and won the prize—a pretty little pin for his tie.

The afternoon wore on, and, almost before the children realized it the hour for supper had arrived. They were not sorry, either, for they all had good appetites.

"Come into the dining room, children," invited Mrs. Bobbsey.

And Oh! such gasps of pleased surprise as were heard when the children saw what had been prepared for them! For Mr. and Mrs. Bobbsey, while not going to any great expense, and not making the children's party too fanciful, had made it beautiful and simple.

The long table was set with dishes and pretty glasses. There were flowers in the centre, and at each end, and also blooms in vases about the room. Then, from the centre chandelier to the four corners of the table, were strings of green smilax in which had been entwined carnations of various colors.

The lights were softly glowing on the pretty scene, and there were prettily shaded candles to add to the effect. But what caught the eyes of all the

children more than anything else were two large cakes—one at either end of the table.

On each cake burned five candles, and on one cake was the name "Flossie," while the other was marked "Freddie." The names were in pink icing on top of the white frosting that covered the birthday cakes.

"Oh! Oh! Oh!" could be heard all about the room. "Isn't that too sweet for anything!"

"I guess they are sweet!" piped up Freddie in his shrill little voice, "'cause Dinah put lots of sugar in 'em; didn't you, Dinah?" and he looked at Dinah, who had thrust her laughing, black, goodnatured face into the dining room door.

"Dat's what I did, honey! Dat's what I did!" she exclaimed. "If anybody's got a toofache he'd better not eat any ob dem cakes, 'cause dey suah am sweet."

How the children laughed at that!

"All ready, now, children, sit down," said Mrs. Bobbsey. "Your names are at your plates."

There was a little confusion getting them all seated, as those on one side of the table found that their name cards were on the other side. But Flossie and Freddie, and Nan and Bert, helped the guests to find their proper places and soon everyone was in his or her chair.

"Can't Snap sit with us, too?" asked Freddie, looking about for his pet, who had done all his tricks well that evening.

"No, dear," said Mrs. Bobbsey. "Snap is a good dog, but we don't want him in the dining room when we are eating. It gives him bad habits."

"Then can't I send him out some cakes?" asked Flossie, for Snap had almost as large a "sweet tooth" as the children themselves.

"Yes, as it is your birthday, I suppose you can give him some of your good things," said Mamma Bobbsey.

"Here, Dinah!" called Freddie to the cook, as he piled a plate full of cakes. "Please give these to Snap."

"Land sakes goodness me alive!" cried Dinah. "Dat suah am queer. Feedin' a dog jest laik a human at a party. I can't bring mahself to it, nohow."

"I'll take 'em out to him," said her husband.

Then the feast began, and such a feast as it was! Mrs. Bobbsey, knowing how easily the delicate stomachs of children can be upset, had wisely selected the food and sweets, and she saw to it that no one ate too much, though she was gently suggestive about it instead of ordering.

"Don't eat too much," advised Freddie to some of the friends who sat near him. "We've got a lot of ice cream coming. Save room for that."

"That's so—I almost forgot," spoke Jimmie Black.

A little later Mrs. Bobbsey said to Dinah:

"I think you may bring in the cream now, and I will help you serve it."

"Yes, ma'am."

"Oh, goodie!" cried Freddie. "Ice cream's coming!" and he waved his spoon above his head.

"Freddie—Freddie!" said his mother, in gentle reproof.

Dinah went out on the back stoop, looked around and came running back to the dining room, where Mrs. Bobbsey was. Dinah's eyes were big with wonder and surprise.

"Mrs. Bobbsey! Mrs. Bobbsey!" she cried. "Suffin's done gone an' happened!"

"What is it?" asked Mamma Bobbsey, quickly. "Is anyone hurt?"

"No'm, but dat ice cream freezer hate jest gone and walked right off de back stoop, an' it ain't dere at all, nohow! De ice cream is all gone!"

The children looked at one another with pained surprise showing on their faces.

The ice cream was gone!

A Coat Button

Astonishment, surprise and disappointment were so great for a few seconds after the discovery that the best part of the party—the ice cream—was gone, that no one knew, what to say. Then Flossie burst out with:

"Are you sure, Dinah? Maybe it fell off the porch."

"Deed an' it didn't, honey gal. I done looked eberywhar fo' dat freezer, an' it's jest gone complete."

"Maybe Snap took it," suggested Freddie, as a last hope. "Once he took my book and hid it. Snap, did you take the ice cream?"

Snap barked and wagged his tail, looking rather pained at being asked such a question.

"No, indeedy, Snap couldn't take off a big freezer like dat," declared Dinah. "It wasn't Snap."

"Then who could it have been?" asked Nan. Everyone had stopped eating while this talk went on. "Who could have taken our ice cream?"

"Dat's what I don't know, honey," answered the colored cook. "Dat's why I comed in heah to tell yo' mamma. I 'spects, Mrs. Bobbsey, dat we'd better phonograph fo' de police."

"Phonograph—I guess you mean telephone; don't you, Dinah?" asked Mrs. Bobbsey, with a smile.

"Yes'm, dat's what I done mean. Or else maybe we kin send mah man Sam down to de station house fo' 'em."

"No, I had better telephone, in case it is necessary. But perhaps I had better take a look out there. Perhaps the man from the store may have set the cream off to one side."

"No'm, he didn't do dat. I took p'ticlar notice where he set it. Dere's a wet ringmark on de porch where de freezer was, 'count of de salty water leakin' out. An' dat wet ringmark am all dat's left ob de cream, dar now!" and Dinah, standing with her hands on her hips, looked at the startled children, whose mouths were just ready for the ice cream.

"Well, I'm going to have a look, anyhow," said Bert. "Come on, Charley. Maybe, after all, that Danny Rugg is up to some of his tricks."

"I'm with you, Bert!" cried Charley. "But we ought to have some sort of a light. It's dark out."

"I'll get my little pocket electric light," said Bert. He had one, and it gave a good light. He went to his room for it.

Flossie and Freddie did not know what to do. That their lovely party should be spoiled by the missing ice cream seemed too bad to be true.

"Mamma, if we can't find this ice cream, can't we buy more?" Flossie wanted to know. "The girls just want some—so bad!"

"And the boys, too," added Freddie.

"Oh, I guess we'll manage to get some fo you, if we can't find this," answered Mrs. Bobbsey. "We may have to wait a little while for it, though."

"Well, we'll have a look," said Bert, as he came down with his little electric lamp. Some of his own particular chums, including Charley Mason, followed him out to the back porch, Dinah was in her kitchen, looking behind tables, under the sink, in the pantry and all about, hoping that, somehow or other, the freezer might have gotten in there. But it was not to be found.

"Well, here's where it stood," said Bert, as he looked at the round, wet mark on the porch where the freezer had set. He flashed his torch on it, and then cried out:

"And look, boys, here are some spots of water that must have leaked from the wooden tub that holds the tin freezer. See, the water has dripped down on each step! This is the way they carried off our ice cream."

The others could see a trail of water drops leading from the stoop down the steps and along the stone walk at the side of the Bobbsey house.

"Now we can follow and see just where they took our cream!" cried Bert. "This is the way Indians used to trail the white settlers."

"Let me come!" cried Freddie, hearing this. "I want to help hunt whoever took our ice cream."

"No, you'd better stay back there," said Bert.

"Why?" his little brother wanted to know.

"Because it might be—tramps—who have it, and there'd be trouble," said Bert.

"Wait until I get my cap pistol!" cried Freddie. "I can scare a tramp with that."

"No, you go back there, and stay in the house," went on Bert. "If we find tramps have it, we'll get a policeman."

"It might be that a tramp did steal up on the steps, and lift off the freezer," said Mrs. Bobbsey. "Bert, be careful," she called to her son, who set off in the darkness with his chums, flashing his electric light from time to time.

"I'll look out!" he called back.

For some distance it was easy to see which way the ice cream freezer had been carried, for there were the marks of the dripping water. Then these stopped about the middle of the sidewalk, and seemed to go over in the grass.

"We can't see 'em now," spoke Charley. "That's too bad."

"Well, we'll keep on this way in a straight line," suggested Bert. "Maybe they took the freezer down back of our berry bushes to eat the cream."

"I hope they left some," said John Anderson, in a mournful sort of voice.

Hurrying on after Bert, the boys looked eagerly about in the darkness for a sign of the missing ice cream. There were not many chances of them finding it, for though Bert's electric torch gave a brilliant light for a short distance, it was not very large.

"What's over there?" asked Charley, pausing and pointing to a patch of blackness.

"An old barn, that we used to use before we had our new one built," answered Bert. "Why?"

"Well, maybe they took the ice cream in there to eat it," went on Charley. "Is it open?"

"Yes, it's never locked. Say, we'll take a look in there, anyhow!" exclaimed Bert. "Come on, fellows!"

He led the way, the others following. As they approached the big, deserted barn Frank Black exclaimed in a whisper:

"I see a light!"

"So do I!" added Will Evans.

"And it's moving around," spoke Charley Mason.

"It's them, all right," decided Bert. "The tramps who took our ice cream are in there, all right!"

"What makes you think they are tramps?" asked Will.

"Well, I'm not sure, of course," admitted Bert. "But we can soon tell. Come on!"

"Are you—are you going up there?" asked Charley.

"Sure! Why not? I think we can scare em away."

The other boys hesitated. Some of them were older than Bert, and when they saw that he was determined to go on, they made up their minds that they would not let him go alone.

"All right—go ahead—we're with you," said Charley.

Bert and the others advanced. As they walked on they could see the light in the barn more plainly. And, as they stopped for a moment they could hear voices talking in low tones.

"More than one," whispered Charley.

"Yes, three or four," said Bert.

They walked ahead again, when suddenly Charley stepped on a stick that broke with a loud snap. In an instant the light in the barn went out, and then could be heard the footsteps of several persons running away.

"There they are!" shouted Bert, dashing forward. "Come on, fellows! We'll get 'em now!"

"That's right!" cried Charley. "Come on, surround 'em!"

Of course this was all said for effect, as the boys had no idea of trying to capture the tramps, or whoever it was that had taken the ice cream. But Bert thought that they could scare the thieves away, for the latter could not tell, in the darkness, how many, nor who were after them.

Flashing his light, Bert dashed ahead, followed by the others. Into the big barn they went, and, just as they entered the main part, they had a glimpse of someone running out of a side door.

"There they go!" cried Charley. "We can catch 'em!"

"No, let 'em go," advised Bert. "Here's our ice cream. Let's see if there's any left. If there is we'll take it back to the party. We might get into trouble if we went after those fellows."

By the gleam of the electric light they could all see the freezer of cream in the middle of the barn floor, near some upturned boxes. A hasty look showed that only a little had been taken out.

"There's plenty left!" said Bert. "We surprised 'em just in time. Now let's get beck to the house."

It was rather a triumphant procession that went back to the home of the Bobbsey twins, carrying the recovered ice cream freezer. And such a shout of delight from Flossie, Freddie and the others as greeted the boys!

"Is there any left?" asked Freddie.

"Plenty," said Bert.

"And did you catch the bad tramps?" Flossie wanted to know.

"They got away," her brother said. "But never mind, we scared them before they had a chance to eat much."

"I 'clar t' goodness sakes alive!" gasped Dinah, when she saw the ice cream freezer carried into her kitchen, "yo' am suttinly a smart boy, Massa Bert—dat's what yo' suah am!"

"Oh, well, the others helped me find it," said Bert, modestly.

As Dinah and Mrs. Bobbsey were dishing out the cream, the colored cook uttered a cry.

"Look out!" she exclaimed. "Dere's suffin black in dere, Mrs. Bobbsey. Maybe it's a stone dem careless tramps put in. Wait 'till I gits it out."

With a longhandled spoon Dinah fished for the black thing, and got it. She put it in a dish, with a small portion of the ice cream, and when the latter had melted, Bert, who was inspecting the object, gave a cry of surprise.

"Why, it's a button—a coat button!" he exclaimed.

"A button? How in the world could that get in there?" asked his mother. "Unless you boys dropped it in when you were carrying the cream."

Bert and the other boys quickly looked at their coats. There were no buttons missing.

"An' it suah wasn't in when de cream come heah," said Dinah. "I knows, fo I took off de kiver an' looked in t' see how hard it were froze. Dat button got in since!"

"Yes, and I think I know how, too!" exclaimed Bert.

"How?" asked Freddie.

"It was dropped in by whoever took the freezer. They must have been eating the cream right out of the can, and maybe they dropped the button in. I'll save it."

"What for?" asked Nan, wonderingly.

"I may be able to find out by it, who took the freezer," went on Bert. "I'm going to look at the coats of all the fellows in school next week, and if I find one with the button like this missing, I'll know what to think."

"Be careful not to accuse anyone wrongly," cautioned his mother.

Bert put the button carefully away, and the party guests were soon eating their ice cream, and discussing the disappearance of the freezer and the finding of it by the boys. Then with the playing of more games, and the singing of songs, the affair came to a close, and goodnights were said.

"We've had a lovely time!" said the boys and girls to Flossie and Freddie, as they left. "Glad you did—come again," invited the small Bobbsey twins.

Even Snap seemed to have enjoyed himself.

And when the house was settling down to quietness for the night, and when Dinah and Mrs. Bobbsey were picking up the dishes, the circus dog marched around like a soldier, with a stick for a gun, and one of the fancy caps, that came in the "surprise" packets, on his head.

When Bert went to bed that night he laid the button found in the ice cream where he would be sure to see it in the morning.

"I'm going to find out whose coat that came off of," he said to himself.

The little Bobbsey twins slept late the next morning, and so did Nan, but Bert was up early.

"I'm going over to the barn, and see if I can tell by looking around it, how many were at our freezer," he said.

But there was nothing there to help him in his search. Some old boxes, placed in a sort of circle, showed where the ones who had taken the ice cream, had rested to eat it.

"They must have had spoons with them," said Bert to himself, as he looked about, "That shows they came all prepared to take our ice cream. So they must have known it was going to be here. Well, I'll see whose coat has a button missing."

It took Bert some days to look carefully at the coats of the various boys in school, who might have been guilty of taking the cream. For a time he had no luck, and then, one afternoon, as he noticed Danny Rugg wearing a coat he seldom had on, Bert walked slowly up to him, clasping the button, with his hand, in his pocket.

His heart beat fast as he noticed that from the middle of Danny's coat a button was gone.

And a glance at the others showed Bert that they were just like the one found in the ice cream freezer.

"I see you've lost a button, Danny," said Bert, slowly.

"Hey?" exclaimed the bully, with a start.

"I see you've lost a button," repeated Bert.

"Yes, I guess it dropped off. Maybe it's home somewhere," said Danny.

"No, it isn't—it's here!" exclaimed Bert, suddenly holding the button out to him.

Thanksgiving

For a moment Danny Rugg just stared at Bert. Then the bully swallowed a sort of lump that came in his throat, and said:

"That isn't my button."

"Isn't it?" asked Bert, politely. "Why, it just matches the others on your coat, and it's got a few threads in the holes, and there are some threads in your coat, just where the button was pulled off. I guess it's your button, all right, Danny."

Danny did not say anything. He looked from the button to Bert, and then at the space on his coat where a button should have been, but where one was missing.

"Well—well," he stammered. "Maybe it is off my coat, but—but how did you get it, Bert Bobbsey?"

"I found it," was the answer. "Don't you want it back?"

He held it out to Danny, who took it slowly.

"Well," went on Bert, with a queer little smile at his enemy, "why don't you ask me where I found it, Danny?"

"Huh! I don't care where you found it. I s'pose you picked it up around the school yard, where I lost it, playing tag with the fellows."

"No, you didn't lose it there," went on Bert, still smiling. "You have another guess coming, Danny."

"Pooh! I don't care where you found it," and Danny was about to turn away.

"Wait a minute," said Bert. "Suppose I say that this button was found in our freezer of ice cream, that you and some other boys took off our stoop the night of Flossie's and Freddie's party, Danny? What about that?"

"It isn't—I didn't—you can't prove anything about me, Bert Bobbsey, and if you go around telling that I took your ice cream, I—"

But Danny did not know what else to say. He was confused and his face was white and red by turns, for he realized that Bert had good proof of what he said.

"Better go slow," advised Bert, calmly. "I don't intend to go around telling what you did. I just want to let you know that I am sure you took our ice cream.

"I—I" began Danny. "You're only trying to fool me!" he exclaimed. "That button wasn't in it at all!"

"Wasn't it?" asked Bert, quietly. "Well, you just ask Charley Mason, or any of the fellows who were at the party, what we found in the freezer, and see what they say."

Danny had nothing to reply to this. Thrusting the button in his pocket he walked off. Bert was sure he had found the boy who had taken the ice cream.

Later, from a boy who had been friends with Danny for some time, but whose father, afterward, decided that his son was getting into bad company, and made him cease playing with the school bully, Bert learned that Danny had planned to take the ice cream freezer off the porch.

He and several boys did this, carrying it to the old barn. They had provided themselves with large spoons, and were having a good time, eating the cream, when they heard the approach of Bert and his friends, and fled, leaving the cream behind.

It was during a dispute as to who should have the right to first dip into the freezer that Danny and a boy named Jake Harkness had a struggle, and in this Danny lost a button which fell into the ice cream without anyone knowing it. The coat Danny wore that night he did not put on again for some time, but when he did Bert saw the missing button.

Danny knew that he had been found out, and for a time he had little to say. But Bert was boy enough not to be able to keep altogether quiet over his discovery. From time to time he would ask Danny:

"Lost any more buttons, lately?"

"You let me alone!" Danny would reply, surlily.

Of course this made talk, the boys wanting to know what it meant, and at last the story came out. This made Danny so angry that he picked several quarrels with Bert. On his part Bert tried to avoid them, but at last he could stand it no longer, and he and Danny came to blows again, Danny striking first.

Bert had been brought up with the idea that fighting, unless it could absolutely be avoided, was not gentlemanly, but in this case he could not get out of it.

He and Danny went at each other with their fists clenched, a crowd of other boys looking on, and urging one or the other to do their best, for both Danny and Bert had friends, though Bert was the best liked.

Danny struck Bert several times, and Bert hit back, once hitting Danny in the eye. Bert's lip was cut, and when the fight was over both boys did not look very nice. But everyone said Bert had the best of it.

"Oh, Bert!" exclaimed his mother, when he came home after the trouble with Danny. "You've been fighting!"

"Yes, mother, I have," he admitted. "I'm sorry, but I couldn't help it. Danny Rugg hit me first. I couldn't run away, could I?"

It was a hard question for a mother to answer. No mother likes to think her son a coward, and that was what the boys would have called Bert had he not stood up to Danny.

"I—I just had to!" continued Bert. "And I beat him, anyhow, mother."

Mrs. Bobbsey cried a little, and then she made the best of it, and bathed Bert's cut lip and bruised forehead. She told his father about it, too, and Mr. Bobbsey, after hearing the account, asked:

"Who won?"

"Well, Bert says he did?"

"Um. Well, I've no doubt but what he did. He's getting quite strong."

"Oh, Richard!" exclaimed Mrs. Bobbsey, in dismay.

"Well, boys will er—have their little troubles," said her husband. "I'm sorry Bert had to fight, but I'm glad he wasn't a coward. But he mustn't fight any more."

Then Mr. Bobbsey sat down to read the evening paper.

The weather was getting cooler. Several nights there had been heavy frosts, and for some time the papers had been saying that it was going to snow, but the white flakes did not sift down from the sky.

Thanksgiving was approaching. It was the end of the Fall term of school, and there were to be examinations to see who would pass into the next higher classes for the Winter season.

Of course in the case of Freddie and Flossie, who were still in the kindergarten, the examinations were not very hard, but they were soon to go into the regular primary class, where they would learn to read. And both the twins were very anxious for this. Bert and Nan had somewhat harder lessons to do, and they had to answer more difficult questions in the examinations.

But I am glad to say that all of the Bobbsey twins were promoted, and Freddie and Flossie came home very proud to tell that when they went back again, after the Thanksgiving holidays, they would be in the primer reading book.

And such preparations as went on for Thanksgiving! Dinah was busy from morning until night, and when the little twins made inquiries about the turkey they were to have Mr. Bobbsey said it would be the biggest he could buy.

"An' I'se gwine t' stuff him wif chestnuts an' oysters," said Dinah. "I tells you what, chilluns, yo' all am suttinly gwine to hab one grand feed."

"I wish everybody was," said Flossie, a bit wistfully. "I hope our cat Snoop, wherever he is, has plenty of milk, and some nice turkey bones."

"I guess he will have," said Mamma Bobbsey, gently.

"I hope all the poor children in our school have enough to eat," said Freddie. "Mr. Tetlow said for us to bring what we could for them."

"And you never told me!" exclaimed Mrs. Bobbsey. "Why didn't you? I would have sent something."

Neither Bert nor Nan had thought to mention at home that a collection would be taken at the school for the poor families in the town. But as soon as Mrs. Bobbsey heard what Freddie said she telephoned to her husband. Mr. Bobbsey went to see Mr. Tetlow, and from him learned that there were a number of families who would not have a very happy Thanksgiving.

Then the lumber merchant gave certain orders to his grocer and butcher, and if a number of poor people were not well supplied with food that gladsome season, it was not the fault of Mr. Bobbsey.

But I am getting a little ahead of my story.

A few days before Thanksgiving Mrs. Bobbsey, with a letter in her hand, came to where the four twins were in the sitting room, talking over what they wanted for Christmas.

"Guess who are coming to spend Thanksgiving with us!" cried Mamma Bobbsey, as she waved the letter in the air.

"Uncle Bobbsey!" guessed Nan.

"Uncle Minturn," said Bert.

The little twins guessed other friends and relatives, and finally Mrs. Bobbsey said:

"Yes, your Uncle Bobbsey and Uncle Minturn are coming, and so are your aunts, and Cousin Harry, Cousin Dorothy and also Hal Bingham, whom you met at the seashore."

"Oh, what a jolly Thanksgiving it will be!" cried the Bobbsey twins.

Mr. Tetlow Asks Questions

Thanksgiving was celebrated in the Bobbsey home as it never had been before. I am afraid if I told you all that went on, of the big, brownroasted turkey, of the piles of crisp turkey, of the pumpkin and mince pies, of the nuts and candies, of the big dishes of cranberry sauce, and the plum pudding that Dinah carried in high above her head—I am afraid if I told you of all these things there would be trouble.

For I am sure you would all be writing to me to ask where the Bobbseys lived, so that you might go and see them, and perhaps spend Christmas with them. Not that they would not be glad to have you, but they have so many friends that their house is sure to be filled over the holidays.

So I will simply say that there was the grandest time ever, and let it go at that.

Uncle and Aunt Bobbsey—Uncle and Aunt Minturn, from the country and seashore, came, with Cousin Dorothy and Cousin Harry then, also, Hal Bingham arrived, and the Bobbsey twins took great delight in showing their former playmates about Lakeport.

"Isn't it lonesome at the seashore now?" asked Nan of Dorothy, as she walked with her cousin about the busy streets of the town.

"Not at all," answered Dorothy. "The sea is never lonesome for me. It always seems to be telling me something, Winter or Summer."

"I love it in the Summer," said Nan, "but in the Winter it seems so cold and cruel."

"That is because you do not know it as well as I do," said Dorothy.

Hal, Harry, and Bert had fine times together. There was no skating, and the little flurry of snow there had been was not enough for coasting, but they had other fun.

"Do your ducks miss our duck Downy?" asked Freddie of his cousin Harry.

"Well, I guess they do," was the laughing answer, for Freddie and Flossie had a pet duck which they took about with them almost as faithfully as they did Snoop. "How is Downy, anyhow?" asked Harry.

"He's fine," answered the little fellow. "Want to see him?" and he took his cousin out to the barn where Downy had a pen all to himself.

"Snoop's gone," said Freddie, "and so is our silver cup, but maybe we'll get that back. It's in a circus."

"In a circus!" cried Harry. "I should think your cat might be in a circus, but not a silver cup."

"We don't know where Snoop is," went on Freddie, "'cause he got away at the time of the circus wreck," and he explained about it. "But we are almost sure the circus fat lady has our cup."

The Thanksgiving holidays came to an end at last and, much to the regret of the Bobbseys, their visitors, old and young, had to go back to their homes.

"But you'll come again at Christmas, won't you?" asked Flossie as she said goodbye.

"We'll try," said her Uncle Bobbsey. "But maybe there won't be room, with Santa Claus and all his reindeers."

"Oh, we'll make room for you," spoke Freddie. "Santa Claus won't stay long."

With a merry peal of laughter the visitors went off to the station, waving farewells. Then came rather a quiet time at the Bobbsey house, as there always is when visitors go. There seems to be a sort of loneliness, when company leaves, no matter how many there are in the family, nor what fun there is. But the feeling soon passes.

"Well, we'll soon be at school again," said Bert, a day or so before the opening of the Winter term. "I wish we'd get some snow. Then it would be more fun."

"Yes," said Freddie. "We could build snow forts and have snowball fights. I wish it would snow hard."

"So do I, so we could ride down hill," said Nan. "Is your big bob nearly done, Bert?"

"No, Charley and I have quite a lot of things to do on it yet, but we're going to work every night after school now, and it will soon be finished."

"I'm going to have skates for Christmas," announced Freddie. "I hope the lake will be frozen over by then."

"I guess it will be," returned Bert. "It's getting colder every night."

The Bobbseys were back at school. For a time Nan and Bert, who were in a higher grade, did not like it so well, as they had a strange teacher, and lessons, too, were more difficult. But they were not children who gave up easily, and soon they were at the head of their class as usual. Their teacher, too, was much nicer than they had thought at first. They had considered her stern, but it was only her way, and soon wore off.

As for Freddie and Flossie, they had advanced but little except in reading, and this opened a new world to them.

"We'll soon be reading books," boasted Freddie, on his way home one day.

"And I'm going to read all about firemen, soldiers and Indians."

"Oh, I'm not," said Flossie. "I'm going to read how to be a nurse, so I can take care of you when you're hurt."

"That will be nice," said Freddie.

One day, at recess, Bert saw Jim Osborne motioning to him in a secret sort of fashion.

"Come on with us," said Jim, who was a new boy in school. "Danny Rugg and some of the rest of us are going to have some sport."

"What doing?" asked Bert.

"Smoking cigarettes back of the coal house. I've got a whole pack."

"No; I don't smoke," said Bert quietly.

"Bah! You're afraid!" sneered Jim.

"Cigarettes can't hurt you. It's only cigars and pipes that do."

"Yes, I admit I am afraid," said Bert. "I'm afraid of getting sick. Besides, I promised my mother I wouldn't smoke until I was twenty-one, and I'm not going to tell a story. Anyhow, I've got an uncle who smokes, and he says cigarettes are worse than a pipe or cigars, and he ought to know."

"Aw, come on!" urged Jim.

"No," said Bert firmly, and he would not go. Jim went off with Danny and some of the other boys, and they were laughing among themselves. Bert felt that they were laughing at him, but he did not mind.

There was to be an examination of the school by some of the members of the Board of Education late that afternoon, and, directly after recess, Mr. Tetlow went to each room to tell the pupils and teachers to get ready for it, and to put certain work on the blackboards, so it could be seen.

When the principal got to the room where Danny Rugg and his particular chums sat, Mr Tetlow, sniffing the air suspiciously, said:

"I smell smoke!"

"I have been noticing it, too," said the lady teacher. "Perhaps the furnace does not work properly."

"It isn't that kind of smoke," went on Mr. Tetlow. "It is tobacco smoke. Have any of you boys been smoking during recess?" he asked sternly, looking across the room.

No one answered. Danny, Jim, and some of the others seemed to be studying their geography lessons very hard.

"I just want to say a word about cigarette smoking," went on Mr. Tetlow, "for that is usually how a boy begins. Of smoking in general, when a boy gets to be a man, I have nothing to say. Some say it is injurious, and others not,

in moderation. But there can be no doubt that for a growing boy to smoke is very harmful. Again I ask if anyone here has been smoking?"

No one replied. The guilty boys bent deep over their books and did not look up.

"Well, I am sure someone here has," said Mr. Tetlow. "I can smell it plainly." He walked down the aisles, looking sharply from one boy to another. If he was sure who were the guilty ones he gave no sign. "And I want to add," said Mr. Tetlow, "that not only is cigarette smoking harmful to the smoker, but it is dangerous. Many fires have been caused in that way. If I find out who of my pupils have been smoking around the school they will be severely punished."

The First Snow

There was considerable talk among the boys in Danny's room after Mr. Tetlow departed. And it was noticed that Danny and some of his particular friends looked around with rather frightened faces, over their shoulders, as they talked among themselves. What they said could not be heard, for they spoke in whispers.

"I hope you weren't one of those boys, Bert," said Nan, as she passed her brother on the way home from school that afternoon. "If you were—"

"You needn't worry," he said, with a smile. "I'm not ready to smoke yet."

"Nor ever, I hope," said Nan, as she turned up her little nose. "It—it smells so."

Nothing more was heard of the smoking matter for several days, and it was about forgotten, when something else came to claim the attention of the Bobbsey twins and their friends.

It was toward the close of school one afternoon, when all the pupils were wishing the hands of the clock would point to letting-out time, that Nan, looking from the window, and away from her arithmetic book, saw a few white flakes of snow sifting lazily down. At once she was all attention, and her lesson was forgotten.

"Oh!" she thought, "it's snowing! And it looks as if it would be a big storm. Oh, I'm so glad!"

Nan did not know all the trouble and misery a big snow storm can cause, so she may be forgiven for wishing for one. She only saw the side of it that meant fun for her and her friends.

The flakes were coming down faster now, and there was about them something which seemed to tell that this storm would be more than a mere flurry or squall, and that it would keep up for some time, making big drifts.

But now a number of other pupils in the room had noticed the storm, and eyes were out of doors rather than on books. The teacher saw that she was not getting the attention of her class, and she understood the reason.

"Now, boys and girls," she said gently, "you can have a good time in the snow after you get out of here. So please give attention to your lessons for a few minutes more. Then you will be finished. Nan Bobbsey, you may go to the board and do the third example."

But Nan was thinking so much of the fun she might have riding down hill, or snowballing with her friends, that she got the example wrong, and had to go to her seat. Nor was Bert any more successful.

Bert was busy thinking about putting a bell and a steering wheel on the new bob he and Charley had made, and when he was asked how many times two and a half went into ten he answered: "Three." He was thinking how many times he would ring the bell on the bob when he came to a street crossing.

When the Bobbsey twins, little and big, came out of school the snow was coming down more thickly. The flakes were not so large, but there were more of them, and they blew here and there in the wind, drifting into piles that would make the shoveling off of walks hard the next day.

There were just about enough of the white crystals on the ground, when the school children came out to make a few snowballs, and this they at once proceeded to do.

Danny Rugg, who had not forgiven Bert for the many times the Bobbsey lad had gotten the best of him, threw a ball at Freddie. But Bert was on the watch, and managed to jump up and catch the white missile in his hand. Then he threw it at Danny, striking him on the neck.

"Here! Where you throwin'?" demanded Danny, in angry tones.

"The same place you are," replied Bert, not a bit afraid. "Good weather for ice cream, Danny," he added, and Danny went off in an angry fashion.

Other boys and girls too, threw the snowballs, but it was in goodnatured fun, and no one was hurt. Some rough boys did use hard snowballs, but they were soon left to play among themselves, while the others amused themselves with soft and fluffy missiles, which, breaking as they hit, scattered the white stuff all over, harming no one.

The girls, while they played at this sport, also indulged in washing the faces of each other. With handsful of snow they rubbed the ears and cheeks of their chums so that there came a healthy glow to the skin.

One or two children, who lived near the school, ran in their yards as soon as the classes were dismissed, and brought out their sleds. But the snow was too thin to pack well and at best the coasting was not good.

"But it soon will be," declared Bert, as he and Charley walked along. "We must finish our bob in a hurry."

"All right. We'll work on it late tonight."

And so the sound of hammer, plane and saw was heard in the old barn, where the sled was being built, until nearly ten o'clock.

"She ought to go very fast!" exclaimed Charley, as they paused to look at their sled.

"I'm sure she will," agreed Bert. "And we'll put some carpet on the top of the main board, for a cushion for some of the girls." His chum agreed that this would be a good plan, and so the bob was made very attractive for the girls.

Bert and Charley took the big sled out for a private trial on a little hill behind the barn without telling anyone about it. They slid down very swiftly, and as they were walking up again Bert said:

"I think we have a fast one all right, Charley."

"I'm sure we have," was the answer.

"It will pass anything on the main hill," went on Bert, and his friend believed him.

The storm kept up all night, and in the morning there was snow enough to suit anyone. Bert laughed as he looked out of the window and saw it.

"There'll be coasting now all right!" he cried, as he saw the big stretch of white over the fields and on the hills. "We can have bob sled races, too."

"Can't we come?" asked Flossie.

"We like sled rides," added Freddie.

"You may come part of the time," answered Bert. "But big sleds aren't for little folks like you."

Not far from the Bobbsey home was a long hill that was most excellent for coasting. It was on this that Charley and Bert had decided to test their new sled on a long stretch.

As they hauled it from the barn where it had been made, and started to pull it to the hill, there were many laughs at the odd homemade affair. For Bert and Charley had done most of the work themselves, and it was rather rough.

"She'll never coast!" cried one boy, with a laugh. He was quite a friend of Danny's.

"Here comes the sled that can, though!" cried another, and Danny himself came into view, pulling a fine, new, big bob after him.

"That's the fastest one on the hill," boasted another lad who was helping Danny pull his sled.

"Well, I think ours is fast, too," said Bert calmly.

"Do you want to race?" asked Danny with a sharp glance at Bert.

"I don't mind," was the answer. It was after school, following the first snow, and the hill was just right for coasting.

"Come on! Come on!" cried a number of boys and girls, as they heard what went on between Danny and Bert. "There's going to be a race on the big hill between the big bobs."

There was much excitement. The sleds were the two largest owned by anyone in the neighborhood, and both were fine ones. Danny had bought his, but Bert and Charley had made theirs, and so, though it was not so fancy, it was stronger. Most eyes were on Danny's sled, for it was painted in bright colors, and brightly varnished. It had a red cushion of carpet on the top, and places at the side to rest one's feet.

The bob of Bert and Charley was built just the same, but it was painted in homemade fashion, and the carpet seat was an old and faded one. But it had a new gong and a fine big steering wheel.

"All ready for the race," cried Danny, as he got his sled in position. "Who's going down with me?"

A number of boys came forward.

"Who's going with Bert and me?" asked Charley, and several others stepped forward.

"Go ahead, if you want to come in last!" sneered Danny, as he got his sled in place. "I'll tell 'em you're coming, Bert."

"All right," was the cool answer. "Get in, boys!"

Soon both sleds were filled, and all was ready for the big race—the first of the season.

A Night Alarm

"Are you all ready?" called Danny to Bert, looking over at the homemade bob, and there was something like contempt in his tone.

"All ready," answered Bert. "I'll start as soon as you give the word."

"We ought to have someone to shove us off," suggested Danny. "It won't be fair if one or the other gets a headstart."

"Hi! He's afraid already!" cried Charley Mason. "He knows we're going to beat!"

"I am not!" retorted Danny. "It will be a walkover for me once I start. But I don't want Bert Bobbsey saying I took advantage of him, after the race is over."

"You needn't be afraid—I won't say so—I won't have to," replied Bert. "All the same I think it would be better if we each had a push. I want to be fair, too."

"Hey, Bert!" called a shrill voice, as the elder Bobbsey lad was looking about for some on the hill to whom he might appeal. "Can't I ride down with you, Bert?"

It was Freddie who called, and he came running up, anxious to take part in the exciting race.

"No, Freddie, not this time," explained Bert kindly. "I want only large boys with me in the race. I'll give you a ride afterward."

"After I beat him, he means," sneered Danny.

"Come on, let's race if we're going to," called some of the boys on Danny's sled.

"Yes; don't stay here all day."

"Get a move on!"

"We'll beat, anyhow, what's the use of racing?"

There were only a few of things that those on the big new sled of Danny's, called to those on Bert's bob. On their part Bert's friends voiced such remarks as:

"We're not so strong on looks, but we'll get there first!"

"We're going to give Danny a tow to the bottom of the hill!"

"He won't know he's moving, once Bert's sled gets started going!"

"Well, what are we going to do?" asked Danny at last. "Shall we shove off ourselves?"

Just then there came along two large boys, Frank Cobb, and his particular chum, Irving Knight.

"What's going on here; a race?" asked Frank.

"It looks that way," said Irving.

"Oh, will you push us off?" begged Bert, appealing to Frank, whose father worked in Mr. Bobbsey's lumber yard.

"Sure we will," answered Frank goodnaturedly. "Take the other sled, Irving," he said to his chum, "and we'll give 'em an even start. Then we'll see which beats, and may the best sled win!"

"That's what I say!" cried Irving.

The two larger boys took their places behind the bobs. They slowly shoved them to the edge of the hill, held them there a moment, and, at a nod to each other, shoved them down evenly.

"Hurray!" cried the crowd of other coasters. "There they go!"

"And Danny's ahead!" said some of his friends.

"No, Bert's sled is!" shouted his admirers.

As a matter of fact, though, both sleds were even at the start. On and on they went very swiftly, for the hill had been worn smooth. Then Bert saw his bob getting ahead a little, and he felt that he was going to win easily.

But he was glad too soon, for, a little later, Danny's sled shot ahead, and for some distance was in the lead.

"Can't you beat him, Bert?" whispered Charley Mason, who sat just behind his chum.

"I hope so," was the answer. "But I can't really do anything. We just have to depend on the sled, you know."

"Steer a little more over to the left," suggested another boy. "It looks smoother there."

"I will," said Bert, and he turned the steering wheel of his bob while Luke Morton, in the rear, pulled hard on the bell, making it clang out a loud warning.

"Look out where you're going, Bert Bobbsey!" warned Danny, looking back.

"You're coming over on my side of the hill!"

"No I'm not. I'm away from the middle even," said Bert. "Besides, I'm behind you."

"I know you are, and you're going to stay there; but I don't want you to run into me."

Bert thought of the time, the winter before, when Danny had run into him, and broken his sled, but he said nothing. He did not want that kind of an accident to be repeated if he could help it.

On, on and on dashed the big bobs, with the crowd on the hill, and a number of coasters scattered along the way, watching anxiously. As soon as Bert had steered over to the left his sled began to go faster, as the snow was packed better there. He was fast catching up to Danny, when one of the boys on that bob, looking back, saw it, and warned the steersman.

"He's coming, Danny," he cried.

"Oh, he is; eh? Well, he won't pass me," and Danny steered his sled over directly in front of Bert's, almost causing Bert to collide with him.

"Shame!" cried some watchers. "That wasn't fair!"

"Let him keep on his own side then," warned Danny.

But this mean trick did Danny little good for, though Bert was forced to go to the right, to avoid crashing into Danny, he, most unexpectedly, found good coasting there, and he shot ahead until his sled was even with that of the bully's.

"Better look out, Danny," warned the boy sitting directly back of him. "He's crowding us fast."

"Oh, it's only a spurt. We'll soon be at the bottom of the hill and win."

On and on came Bert's bob, the Flier. It was a little ahead of Danny's now, and the latter, seeing this, steered over, thinking the going was better there.

"Look out!" warned Bert. "Who's crowding over now?"

"Well, I've got a right here!" snarled Danny.

But Bert knew his rights also, and would not give away. He held to his place, and Danny dared not come too close. Then, as Bert found himself on smooth, hardpacked snow, he steered as straight as he could. More and more ahead of Danny he went, until he was fully in front of him.

"We're going to win! We're going to win!" cried Bert's friends. "We're going to win the race!"

Danny was wild with anger. He steered his sled over sharply, hoping to get on the same track as was Bert and so pass him. But it was not to be. Danny took too sudden a turn, and the next instant his bob overturned, spilling everyone off.

There was a cry of surprise at the accident, and some of those on Bert's sled looked back. Bert himself looked straight ahead as a steersman always should.

"Danny's upset!" cried Charley.

"I'm sorry!" said Bert. "Now he'll claim the race wasn't fair."

And that is what Danny did when he picked himself up, and walked down to meet Bert, whose bob got safely to the foot of the hill, and so won the race.

"Aw, I'd have beaten if you hadn't gotten in my way so I had to steer over," cried Danny.

"Don't talk that way now," said Irving, who, with Frank Cobb had come to the end of the hill. "Bert beat you fair and square."

"Aw, well," grumbled Danny.

"I'll race over again, if you like," offered Bert.

"Yes, and do the same thing," grumbled Danny. "I will not. I know my sled is the best."

But few others, save those who hoped for a ride on it, agreed with the bully, and Bert's homemade bob was held to be champion of the hill.

Then came many more coasts, Bert giving Nan and Flossie and Freddie, and a number of their little girl and boy friends, several rides.

Until late that evening the coasting kept up, and Bert and Charley were congratulated on all sides for the fine bob they had made. And what fun Bert had home after supper, telling of how he had won the race!

It was in the middle of the night, when the Bobbsey household was awakened by the ringing of fire bells. They all heard the alarm, and as Papa Bobbsey counted the number, he said to his wife:

"That must be near here. Guess I'll look. It's a windy night and a fire in my lumber yard would be very bad."

As he went to the window he saw a glare on the sky in the direction of the lake.

"It is near here!" he said. "The engines are going past our house! I'd better take a look."

"Can I come?" asked the little "Fat Fireman" from his cot. "Take me, papa!"

Who Was Smoking?

MR. BOBBSEY laughed, though he was worried about the fire. It seemed so odd for Freddie to want to go out in the cold, dark night.

"Not this time, my Fat Fireman!" said Freddie's papa. "It may be only a pile of rubbish on fire. I'll tell you about it when I come back."

"Where does it seem to be?" asked Mrs. Bobbsey.

"Down near the lake," answered her husband. "I'm afraid, he added in a lower voice, that it may be our boathouse. It seems to be about there."

"Oh, I hope not!" she exclaimed. "Still, better that than our own house."

"If it's near the lake, papa," said Flossie who heard part of what her father said, "it will be easy to put it out, for there is plenty of water."

"Pooh! engines have their own water!" exclaimed Freddie, who had rather hazy notions as to how fire engines work. He was getting over his disappointment about not being allowed to go with his father, and had again cuddled down in his warm crib.

Another engine dashed by the Bobbsey house, and the ringing of the alarm bell increased. The voices and footsteps of many persons, as they rushed on to the blaze, could also be heard, and there resounded the cry of:

"Fire! Fire! Fire!"

Bert, who had been aroused with the others of the household, was dressing in his room. He felt that his father would let him go to the fire. At any rate he intended to be all ready when he made his request, so as not to cause delay.

"Are you going, Bert?" asked Nan, as from her room, next to that of her brother, she heard him moving around.

"I am, if father will take me," he said.

"It's too cold for me!" Nan exclaimed with a shiver, as she went back in bed again. She had gotten up to peer from the window at the red glare in the sky.

From the third floor, where Dinah slept, the colored cook now called down:

"Am anybody sick, Mrs. Bobbsey? What am de mattah down dere?"

"It's a fire, Dinah!" answered her mistress.

"Oh good land a'massy! Don't tell me dat!" she cried. "Sam! Sam! Wake up. De house is on fire an' you'se got t' sabe me!"

"No, no, Dinah!" cried Mrs. Bobbsey, to calm the cook. "It isn't this house. It's down by the lake. If you look out of your window you can see it."

Dinah hurried across to her window, and evidently saw the reflection of the blaze, for she exclaimed:

"Thank goodness it ain't yeah! Mah goodness, but I suah was skarit fo' a minute!"

By this time Mr. Bobbsey had dressed, and had started downstairs. Bert came out of his room, also ready for the street.

"May I come, father?" he asked.

"Well, I declare!" exclaimed Mr. Bobbsey, in surprise. "So you got dressed too, did you?"

"Yes, sir. May I come?"

Mr. Bobbsey hesitated a moment, and then, with a smile, said:

"Well, I suppose so, since you are all ready. I'm taking Bert," he called to his wife. "Freddie, you'll have to be the Fat Fireman while I'm gone, and look after the house."

"That's what I will," said Freddie, "and if any sparks fly over here I'll throw the bath room sponge on 'em!"

"Good!" cried Mr. Bobbsey, and then, he and Bert hurried out.

The fire was now larger, as they could see when they got out in the street. There was no wind and the flames went straight up in the air. There were not many buildings down by the lake, only some boat shelters and places like that. The Bobbsey's boathouse was a fine large one, having recently been made bigger as Mr. Bobbsey was thinking of buying a new motor boat.

Mr. Bobbsey and his son hurried on, following the crowd that filled the street leading to the lake. Several gentlemen knew the lumber merchant, and called to him.

"I guess you're glad this isn't your lumber yard," said one.

"Yes, indeed," was the answer. "I had a little fire there once, and I don't want another. But I'm afraid this is some of my property just the same."

"Is that so?"

"Yes, it looks to be my boathouse."

"So it does!" cried another man.

"Oh, father!" cried Bert. "Our nice boathouse!"

"Well, the firemen may save it," said Mr. Bobbsey. "We will hope so, anyhow," he added.

They had not gone on much farther before Mr. Bobbsey and Bert could see that it was indeed their boathouse on fire. One side was all ablaze, and the flames were slowly, but surely, eating their way over the whole place. But two

engines were now pumping streams of water on the fire, and they might put it out before too much damage was done.

Mr. Bobbsey rushed forward, and, as the policemen and firemen knew him, they let him get close to the boathouse.

"You stay here, Bert," said Mr. Bobbsey to his son.

"Where are you going?" Bert wanted to know.

"I'm going to see if we can save any of the boats."

There was a sailing craft, a number of rowboats, and a small gasoline launch in the boathouse. They had been stored away for the winter.

"Come on, men!" cried Mr. Bobbsey, as he saw some of his workmen in the crowd. "Help me save the boats!"

All rushed forward willingly, and, as there was part of the place where the flames had not yet reached, they could make their way into the house. They began lowering the boats into the icy water, while the firemen played the several lines of hose on the flames.

The third engine was now working, and so much water was pumped that even a larger fire could not have stood it for very long. The blaze began to die down, and when Mr. Bobbsey and his men were about to lower the gasoline launch into the icy water the chief ran up, saying:

"You don't need to do that! We've got the fire under control now. It will soon be out."

"Are you sure?" asked the lumber merchant.

"Yes. You can see for yourself. Leave the boat there. It will be all right."

Mr. Bobbsey looked, and was satisfied that the larger part of the boathouse would be saved. So he and his men stopped their work; and went outside to cool off.

A little later the fire was practically out, but one engine continued to throw water on the smouldering sparks. The crowd began to leave now, for there was nothing more to see, and it was cold.

"My!" exclaimed Bert as his father came back to where he had left his son, "it didn't take long to settle that fire."

"No, we have a good fire department," replied Mr. Bobbsey.

The fire chief came up to Mr Bobbsey, who expressed his thanks for the quick work of the firemen.

"Have you any idea what started the fire, Mr. Bobbsey?" asked the chief. "Was the boathouse in use?"

"No," was the answer. "It had been closed for the winter some time ago—in fact as soon as the carpenters finished making the changes. No one was in it as far as I know."

"Then how do you account for this?" asked the chief, as he held out a box partly filled with cigarettes. "I picked these up in the living room," he went on, for the boathouse had one room carpeted, and fitted with chairs and tables, and electric lights where the family often spent evenings during Summer.

"You found those cigarettes in the living room of the boathouse?" asked Mr. Bobbsey.

"I did; and the question is who was smoking?" went on the chief. "In my opinion the end of a cigarette thrown aside, or perhaps a lighted match dropped in some corner, started this fire. Who was smoking?"

A Confession

The chief handed Mr. Bobbsey the half-emptied cigarette box. Mr. Bobbsey turned it over and over in his hand, as though trying to learn to whom it belonged.

"They are something I never use," he said. "I don't suppose we could tell, from this, who had it?"

"No," and the chief shook his head. "It's a common kind, and a good many of the stores sell 'em. A good many of the boys smoke 'em, too—that's the worst of it," and he looked at Bert a bit sharply.

"Oh, you needn't be afraid for my boy!" exclaimed Mr. Bobbsey hastily. "I have Bert's promise that he won't smoke until he's man, and perhaps he won't want to then."

"Good!" exclaimed the chief heartily; "That's what I like to hear. But it's as certain as guns is, and nothing more certain than them, that some one was smoking in your boathouse, and set fire to it. And I wish we could find out who it was."

"So do I!" exclaimed Mr. Bobbsey. "If only to teach them a lesson on how dangerous it is to be careless. Well, I suppose we can't do anything more," and he sighed, for half the beautiful boathouse was in ruins.

Mr. Bobbsey and Bert were soon at home, telling the news to the folks.

Freddie's eyes opened wide in surprise as he listened to the account of how the firemen had put out the fire.

"Oh, I wish I could have been there!" he cried. "I could have helped."

"What caused the fire?" asked Mrs. Bobbsey of her husband, when the children had gone to bed again.

"Some boys—or some one else smoking cigarettes, the chief thinks. We found a half-emptied box."

In her room Nan heard the word "cigarettes" and she wondered if her brother could be at fault, for she remembered he had told her how once some boys had asked him to go off in secret and smoke.

Mr. Bobbsey was up early, for he wanted to see by daylight what damage the fire had done, and he also wanted to see the insurance company about the loss. The beautiful boathouse looked worse in the daylight than it had at night, and the neat living room, where some of the Bobbseys had spent many happy hours, while others of them were out in the boats, was in ruins.

The fire chief came down while Mr. Bobbsey was there, and they talked matters over. The chief said he would send one of his men around to the different stores that sold cigarettes, to try and learn if boys had purchased any that afternoon, for it was against the law to sell cigarettes to anyone under sixteen years of age.

One afternoon Danny's father, Mr. Rugg, came home unexpectedly, and, wanting something that was out in his barn went to get it. As he entered the place he heard a scramble of feet, some excited whispers, and then silence. He was sure that some one was in the place and had run to hide.

"Who's there?" called Mr. Rugg sharply. There was no answer, but he listened and was sure he heard some one in the little room where the harness was kept.

He walked over to the door, and tried to open it. Some one on the inside was holding it, but Mr. Rugg gave a strong pull, and the door flew open. To the surprise of Mr. Rugg he saw his son Danny, and a number of boys, hiding there, and the smell of cigarette smoke was very strong.

"Danny!" exclaimed his father sternly, "what does this mean?"

"We—were—playing!" stammered Danny. "Playing hide and seek."

"And to play that is it necessary to smoke?" Mr. Rugg asked sharply.

"We—we aren't smoking," answered Danny.

"Not now, but you have been. I can smell it plainly. Go into the house, Danny, and these other boys must go home. If I find them smoking in my barn again I shall punish them. You might have set it on fire."

Danny had nothing to say, indeed, there was little he could say. He had been caught in the act.

The other boys slunk off, and Danny went into the house, his father following.

"Danny, I am very sorry to learn this," said Mr. Rugg. "I did not know that you smoked—a boy of your age!"

"Well, I never smoked much. Lots of the fellows smoke more than I do."

"That is no excuse. It is a bad habit for a boy. You may go to your room. I will consider your case later."

From then on Mr. Rugg did some hard thinking. He began "putting two and two together" as the old saying has it. He remembered the Bobbsey boathouse fire. On that occasion Danny had come in late, and there had been the smell of smoke on his clothes.

Mr. Rugg went to his son's room. A search showed a number of empty cigarette boxes, and cigarette pictures, and the boxes were all of the same kind—the kind that had been found in the halfburned boathouse.

Danny was accused by his father of having been smoking in the boathouse just before the fire, and Danny was so miserable, and so surprised at being caught in the barn, that he made a full confession. Tearfully he told the story, how he and some other boys, finding the boat house unlocked, for some unknown reason, had gone in, and smoked to their heart's content.

They did not mean to cause the fire, and had no idea that they were to blame. One of the boys was made ill by too much smoking, and they all hurried away.

But they must have left a smouldering stump of cigarette in some corner, or a carelessly thrown match, that started the blaze. Then, when the fire bells sounded, and they learned what had happened, Danny and all the boys promised each other that they would keep the secret.

"Well, Danny, I can't tell you how sorry I am," said Mr. Rugg, when the confession was over. "Sorry not only that Mr. Bobbsey's boathouse was burned, but because you have deceived me, and your good mother, and smoked in secret. I feel very badly about it."

Danny did, too, for though he was not a very good boy, his heart was in the right place, and with a little more care he might have been a different character. There was, however, hope for him.

"You must be punished for this," went on Mr. Rugg, "and this punishment will be that you are not to have the motor boat I promised you for next Summer. Perhaps it will be a lesson to you."

Danny wept bitterly, for he had counted very much on having this boat. But it was a good lesson to him. Mr. Rugg also told the fathers of the other boys whom he caught with his son, and these boys were punished in different ways.

Mr. Rugg also informed Mr. Bobbsey how the boathouse had been set afire, and expressed his sorrow. And so the mystery was cleared up.

The Fat Lady's Letter

"Well," remarked Nan Bobbsey, a few days after it had become known that Danny Rugg was to blame for the fire in the boathouse, "I wish we could find out, as easily as we found out about Danny, who has our cat Snoop."

"So do I," added Flossie. "Poor Snoop! I do miss him so much."

"So do I!" exclaimed Freddie. "But Snap is a nice dog, and I guess I like dogs better than cats, anyhow."

"Why, Freddie Bobbsey!" cried Nan.

"Don't you love Snoop any more?"

"Oh, yes, 'course I do, but then he isn't here to be loved, and Snap is."

"Yes, I guess that does make a difference," admitted Nan. "I wonder if papa wouldn't let us go down to the railroad office and inquire once more about him? Maybe, as it's getting cold weather now, Snoop will come in from the fields where he may have been staying ever since the railroad wreck."

"Let's ask," cried Freddie, always ready for action.

It was Saturday, and there was no school. Bert had gone off coasting on his new bob, but Nan did not want to go, her mother having asked her to stay and help with the dusting. But now the little bit of housework was over, and Nan was free.

"We'll go down to papa's office," she said to Flossie and Freddie, "and ask him if we can go to the railroad. I know one of the ticket agents and he can tell us of whom to ask about our cat."

Mrs. Bobbsey had no objections, and soon, with Flossie and Freddie at her side, Nan set off for her father's office in the lumber yard. The smaller twins were delighted.

"And maybe we can find our silver cup, too," suggested Freddie, as they trudged along in the snow, now and then stopping to make a white ball, which he threw at the fence or telegraph pole.

"The fat lady has our cup—I'm sure of that," said Flossie.

"Well, we can ask papa if he has heard from the circus people," suggested Nan.

Mr. Bobbsey was rather surprised to see his three children come into the office, but he was glad to meet them, for it made a break in his day's work. After a little thought he said they might go to the railroad office to inquire about Snoop. Nan and her brother and sister went in a trolley car, and were soon at the depot.

But to their disappointment there was no news of Snoop. The fat, black cat seemed to have completely disappeared.

"I've had the switchmen and trackmen keep a lookout for some time past," the agent told Nan, for Mr. Bobbsey did a large business in shipping lumber over the railroad, and many of the men were his friends. "One of the switchmen near where the wreck was, caught a lot of cats, that must have been living out in the fields all Summer," went on the agent, "but they were all sorts of colors. None was pure black, so I knew they could not be yours. I'm sorry."

"Yes, so are we," replied Nan. "Well, I guess Snoop is lost for good. He has been away a long time now."

On the way back to Mr. Bobbsey's office, the trolley car got off the track, on account of so much snow on the rails, and the children spent some time watching the men get it back, the electricity from the wire and rails making pretty flashes of blue fire.

"What luck?" asked Mr. Bobbsey, as the three came in his private office, their faces shining and red with the glow of winter.

"None," said Nan sadly. "Snoop is gone."

"Have you heard from the circus fat lady yet, papa?" asked Flossie.

"Yes, we want our cup back," added her brother.

"No word yet," answered Mr. Bobbsey. "That circus is traveling all over Cuba, and the letters I sent never seem to catch up to them. However, I am sending one on ahead now, to a city where they will soon give a show. The fat lady will find it there waiting for her, and she may answer then."

And with this the children had to be content. Getting back home, Flossie and Freddie took out their sleds and went for a coast on a small hill, not far from their home. This was where the smaller children had their fun, leaving the larger hill for the bigger girls and boys.

"Well, after this I think we all need something to cheer us up," said Papa Bobbsey, who came home from the office early that day.

"Oh, have you got something good?" asked Nan, for she saw a queer little twinkle in her father's eyes, and she knew that this generally meant a treat of some kind.

"I have some good news, if you would like to hear it," he said, as he drew a letter from his pocket.

"Is it to tell that some of our friends are coming to see us?" asked Bert.

"Well, yes, I think you will call it a visit from a friend—at least part of it," said Papa Bobbsey. "Now listen. This is a letter from the fat lady in the circus."

"What!" cried Flossie, "—the one who has our cup?"

"The same," said Mr. Bobbsey with a smile. "And she has more than your cup. Listen," and he read the letter.

It was too long to put it all in here, but it went on to say how the fat lady really had the valuable silver cup belonging to the twins.

"They loaned it to me to drink from," she wrote, "and when the train stopped so suddenly, there was so much confusion that I put it in my valise by mistake. I have had it ever since and have been wondering how I could send it back to you. The circus went to Cuba soon after that, and has been traveling around that island ever since. I have only just received your last letter asking me about the cup, or I would have answered before. If you will send me directions how to ship the cup to you I shall be very glad to return it."

"Oh goodie!" cried Freddie. "We'll have our nice cup again!"

"Is that all in the letter, papa?" asked Flossie.

"No, not quite," he said. "I'll read a little more," and he read:

"When our circus was wrecked we lost a valuable trick dog. He could play soldier, say his prayers, turn somersaults, and do a number of tricks. The ringmaster feels very badly about losing him, and has tried to locate him, but without success. If you should hear of anyone near you having such a dog we would be much obliged if you would send him to us as he belongs to the circus."

There was a moment of silence after Mr. Bobbsey read this, and then Freddie said:

"Why that must be Snap—our pet dog! Oh, papa you won't give him back to the circus; will you?"

Snap and Snoop

All of the Bobbsey twins—Nan, Bert, Flossie and Freddie—looked so serious over the prospect of losing Snap that Mr. Bobbsey had to laugh. He just couldn't help it.

"Well, I don't see anything to make fun over," said Nan, with a little pout.

"Why, you all act as though you had lost your best friend—or were going to."

"Well, Snap is one of our best friends, aren't you Snap?" said Freddie.

"Still, if he belongs to the circus I don't see but what I'll have to send him back," went on Mr. Bobbsey, slowly.

At this Flossie burst into tears, and Mrs. Bobbsey, putting her arms about the little girl, said to her husband:

"Are you in earnest Richard? Don't tease the child."

"I'm not, Mary. The fat lady wrote just that. I believe the dog we have does belong to the circus."

"Then we'll have to give him up I suppose," and Mrs. Bobbsey sighed, for she had grown very much attached to the fine animal.

"Well, we won't have to send him back right away," said Mr. Bobbsey. "I will have to get more particulars. But I did not finish the fat lady's letter."

"What! Is there more news in it?" asked Nan.

"Listen," said Mr. Bobbsey, as he went on reading:

"We are sorry about losing our trick dog," the fat lady wrote, "but I picked up a big black cat when I walked out of the train. I brought him to Cuba with me, and I am teaching him tricks. He may be as valuable as our dog was."

"A black cat!" cried Nan.

"It's our Snoop!" shouted Freddie, "yes, that's it! The fat lady has our cat as well as our cup. Oh, papa, make her give back our Snoop!"

Mr. Bobbsey laughed.

"You see how it is," he said. "She has our cat, and we have their dog. We'll have to give up our dog to get our cat."

The Bobbsey twins had not thought of this before. They looked strangely at one another.

"Papa!" cried Freddie, jumping up and down in his excitement, "can't we keep both—the circus dog and our cat? Oh, do please, let us."

"But maybe Snap would fight Snoop," said Flossie. "We wouldn't want that."

Freddie thought for a moment.

"I don't believe he would," he said at last.

"Well," said Papa Bobbsey, after a bit, "I'll see what I can do. I'll write to the fat lady, telling her how to ship your silver cup, and also how to send Snoop. And I'll ask if we can buy Snap. How will that do?"

"Fine!" cried all the Bobbsey twins at once, and they made a rush for Mr. Bobbsey, hugging and kissing him.

The letter was sent to the fat lady, and then came a time of anxious waiting. Never before had the children seemed to care so much for Snap.

One day a letter came, saying that the silver cup had been sent, and also Snoop, the cat.

"But what about Snap, papa?" asked Nan.

"Does she say the circus will sell him?"

"No, the man who owns him is away for a few days. When he comes back he will let me know. But, anyhow, you will have your cup and cat back."

"But we want Snap, too!" said Flossie.

Several more days passed. They lengthened into a week, and still no news came from where the circus was: All the Bobbsey twins could hope was that their cat and cup were on the way, and that the man who owned Snap would consent to sell him.

The twins did not feel much like having fun. There was a warm spell, and all the snow had melted.

One day an express wagon stopped in front of the Bobbsey house.

It was a Saturday, and there was no school, and, as it happened, all four of the twins were in.

"Two boxes for you, Mrs. Bobbsey," said the driver, as he opened his receipt book. "I'll bring them in while you sign."

The man came up the walk with two boxes. One was small, and the other larger, with slats on one end. And from this box came a peculiar noise.

"Listen!" cried Bert.

"It's a cat!" shouted Freddie.

"It's Snoop—our Snoop!" cried Flossie.

Quickly the boxes were carried into the house. Bert got a hammer and screw driver and soon had opened the one containing the black cat. Snap, the dog, walked slowly into the room.

"Oh dear!" cried Flossie as she saw him, "now maybe they'll fight!"

"I'll hold Snap," volunteered Freddie.

"Come on, Snoop! Come out!" cried Bert, as he pried off the last slat.

"Meouw!" cried Snoop, as he came slowly out of the box in which he had ridden from Cuba.

Out walked the black cat. He looked about him strangely for a moment, and then began to purr, and rubbed up against Flossie's legs.

They all looked anxiously at Snap. The dog glanced at the cat, stretched lazily and wagged his tail. Snoop came over to him, and the two animals sniffed at each other, Mrs. Bobbsey holding Snap by the collar. Then, to the surprise of all, Snoop rubbed against the legs of the dog, and, on his part, Snap, wagging his tail in friendly, welcoming fashion, put out his red tongue and licked Snoop's fur.

"He's kissing Snoop! He's kissing Snoop!" cried Freddie.

"Yes, they love each other!" exclaimed Flossie. "They are not going to fight! Oh, how glad I am!" and she danced in delight.

"Oh, if only we can keep Snap now," said Nan, while Mrs. Bobbsey, satisfied that the two animals would be friends, had opened the other express box. It contained the twins' silver cup, so long missing.

Mr. Bobbsey came home soon after that his face was smiling.

"Oh, papa!" Flossie greeted him, "Snoop came, and Snap kissed him!"

"May we keep Snap, papa?" asked Freddie.

"Yes," was Mr. Bobbsey's answer. "I have a letter from the circus man, and he will sell Snap to me. I have already sent the money. And there is another letter from the fat lady, telling about some of the new tricks she taught Snoop, so you can make him do them."

"Oh! Oh! Oh!" cried the Bobbsey twins in firelight, as they looked at their two pets.

"What lots of things have happened since we came back from the seashore," said Nan, little later. "I wonder if the rest of the Winter will be as lively as this first part has been?"

"Maybe," said Bert with a smile.

And whether it was or not you may learn by reading the next volume of this series, to be called: "The Bobbsey Twins at Snow Lodge," in which we will once more hear of the doings of Flossie, Freddie Nan and Bert.

After reading the fat lady's second letter the twins got Snoop to do some of the tricks the cat had learned. He was not as smart at them as Snap was at his, but then cats never do learn to do tricks as well as do dogs.

Still everyone agreed that the fat lady had done her training well. As for Snap, he and Snoop became firmer friends every day, and often the cat went to sleep on Snap's back, or between his forepaws as he lay stretched out in front of the fire.

And the silver cup, which, with Snoop, had gone on such a long journey, was put back in its place on the mantle, to be admired by all.

Now my little story has come to an end, but I hope you children who have read it will care to hear more of the Bobbsey twins and the things they did. So I will say goodbye for a while, trusting to meet you all again.

Made in the USA
Middletown, DE
27 June 2020